In memory of my Pine Knoll Shores
Golden Girl Investors

BEGIN AGAIN, QUINN

Karen Dodd

Carol—
I bet you know someone
who reminds you of Quinn
or one of her friends —
"Stay Safe."
Karen Dodd
4-7-2012

Published by Karen Dodd

New Bern, NC
ISBN#9780-9707197-5-1
Begin Again, Quinn

Cover art: Barry and Vonceal Kubler's Southport home by Karen Dodd with the assistance of Carl Hultman.

Other books in print by this author include
Carolina Comfort 3rd Edition ISBN# 970719744
Carolina Comfort II ISBN# 970719728
Down East on Nelson Island ISBN# 970719737

Begin Again, Quinn

PROLOGUE

As Margaret Byrd falls to her death, the tingling in her shoulder prevents her arms from reaching out to break her descent. She hears the crack in her neck as she tumbles against the hand railing. Flashes of Ginny on her wedding day and Ryan fishing with his father on a nearby beach shuffle by like pages from the family album. She sees her late husband reach for her.

"Birdie!" He calls to her and then vanishes, like the rest of her family.

A confused and broken Birdie stares up at her killer outlined by the night sky. He guzzles the rest of his drink, tosses the ice cubes off the side of the deck and slides the glass into his jacket pocket. Without looking back, he turns and walks away.

Blood seeps through her newly permed hair. Her fingers dig into the cooling beach sand. The brightly painted, now chipped, nails match her lips, Fuchsia Dawn. She bought the polish for her special date earlier in the afternoon. Within seconds, darkness cloaks her mind.

The next morning, police find Margaret Byrd's sandals neatly placed beneath a canvas deck chair. A near-empty bottle of bourbon, cool water in an ice bucket and one cut glass tumbler sit on a table. A lipstick kiss taints the rim of the glass, Fuchsia Dawn.

Karen Dodd

ONE

Since retiring to my hometown, a coastal North Carolina community, Sunday morning resembles every other day of the week, except my newspaper is fatter and I wear a dress to the early church service. While I'm in church, Danny Bridges, sometime organist and fulltime Bridges Book Store proprietor, goes fishing in search of whatever's running. This morning, he shows up at my front door about ten o'clock.

"Quinn Winslow," he hollers, "I got you some shrimp if you want them. They're the first of the season."

I hurriedly pull on my elastic-waist shorts and a cover-it-all tee shirt. I brush my bangs out of my eyes as I walk down the hall toward him. "Morning, Danny." I push open the screen door.

He kicks off his boat shoes on the front porch and carries in a twenty-gallon cooler full of fresh-caught, bug-eyed, long-antennaed gray shrimp, the kind I love. Danny follows me into the kitchen. His Hawaiian print shirt matches my newly painted lime walls perfectly. The khaki cargo shorts leave a lot to be desired, but beggars can't be choosey about their fish monger's clothes.

"Nice color green. If I had known you had that shirt, I'd have saved hours comparing paint chips when I went looking at colors for my kitchen walls."

"Sorry I missed the endeavor." His deep voice mocks me as he backs up to hold a shoulder against one wall for comparison.

I pull on yellow rubber gloves and warn, "Don't bring me fresh shrimp if you're not staying to finish the task."

He taps the ice chest with a finger. "I'm staying." The bleached white hairs on his arm betray the hours he spends in the sun. Lining my farmhouse sink with newspaper, Danny hoists the cooler and dumps out the shrimp along with seaweed, slugs and trash fish that tangled in his net.

The smell of the ocean fills my nostrils; I reclaim the pride of being a fisherman's daughter. Holding my gloved hands up like a surgeon. "You want a pair of these or are you gonna pop off the heads with your naked thumbs?"

"You got another pair?"

"Uh-huh." I tap the white bead-board cabinet door with my bare toe.

He helps himself to the extra rubber gloves under the sink. "Where you keep the freezer bags? I may as well open a bunch before we start." Danny heads to the pantry where I point, grabs a box of super Ziplocs and then pulls a stool over to the sink to join me.

"So, no organ playing today? You must miss a lot of church music during shrimp season."

He shrugs. "I don't need the extra money anymore. I only do it to keep the old fingers in step with the notes on a page." His fingers dance across the countertop as he mimes a tune. He picks up another couple of shrimp and heads them, twice as fast as I do.

Danny and I went to the same grade school over fifty years ago, where he tried to peek under my dress as I swung hand over fist across the monkey bars. I bumped into Danny after I moved back home seven months ago.

Danny calls and visits whenever he's not working, as if he's trying to fan up some love embers between us. Being around any man makes me self-conscious. Since my abusive marriage, I squirm at the thought of having a significant other. I am not interested in a husband, be it Danny or -- my neighbor, Charles Goodwin, a consternating retired colonel who lives next door.

"Did you get in the latest Pat Conroy yet?"

Danny keeps me supplied with reading material as well as seafood. "Next week, for sure." He takes a deep whiff of the fishy odor. "*Mmm*, unless you grow up on the coast, you can't fully appreciate the smell of fresh shrimp on wet newspaper." Graying auburn hair falls on his forehead. A fleck of shrimp shell is stuck to his cheek where pale freckles trail across his face. He taps a wet spot on the obituaries where I circled Margaret Byrd's death notice. "Did you know her?"

I shake my head. "Grier mentioned her. When I saw the name, I circled it."

"Hmm, if I didn't know better I'd think someone was helping old people die around here."

"What a thing to say!"

"I haven't got proof, but there seems to be an increase in accidental deaths in this neighborhood."

"We fall more as we get older."

"Don't try to smooth it over. I did Mrs. Byrd's memorial service. A couple of grown children, from out of state and a few friends, including your cousin Grier, attended the memorial service. It's funerals with so few people attending started me thinking."

"By the way, I hear Mrs. Byrd fell after one too many." He curves his fingers, as if he's holding a glass and tips his head back, then licks his sun-chapped lips. "Maybe she had a little push after a couple of drinks."

"Don't go spreading sad tales about the dead, Danny." I admit if I want to hear fresh gossip, I stop in his bookstore for a cup of coffee.

"She was one of Grier's friends." I frown, trying to remember if my cousin ever introduced us. "I didn't know her." I snap another handful of shrimp into a bag. "Older people, like us, need to be more careful. We're not as quick or flexible as we once were." I plow my fingers through the shells in the sink. "People need to stay active." I silently thank my lucky stars my work the past thirty years kept me agile. "This will all be cleaned and in the freezer by lunchtime. Stay for lunch. I'll throw some in boiling water and make us a salad."

Being silly, he says, "I'se hoping you'd ask me, Miss Quinn." He flutters pale lashes over his green eyes, giving me a lop-sided grin. For a moment, he's the kid I remember and not a sixty-year-old man hitting on me.

When we were kids, we worked at Captain Tony's Restaurant in Morehead City. I started working as a waitress when I was fifteen. Danny hustled in the kitchen. He was one of their best hushpuppy makers until he left for college. However, I came out the better cook.

With a slime-free backhand, I return his smile as I wipe bangs off my forehead. Shrimp entrails track across the sink and my gloved hands. My roly-poly figure sausaged into cotton knit shirt and pants, now smelling like Neptune's bounty, hasn't fazed Danny's attraction to me. If seafood's a part of your soul, I guess this could be romantic stuff.

"Back to the Margaret Byrd issue, for a minute," he says, "you know in the past eighteen months, it seems bizarre accidents kill a lot of people. No one shows up for the memorial services either. It's like all their friends or families are dead, too."

"You must be exaggerating." His comments bother me. "Let's change the subject. You are muddling my mind. I have a favor to ask." Danny knew Matt, my former husband, had a violent temper. "Have I mentioned I volunteer at Help & Hands, the Domestic Abuse Center?" He nods. "I know a woman who passed our basic job skills class. She's good with people."

"People need training. Half the time I get someone in, they can't fill out the job application much less make change."

"She's ready to work. Could you use someone part-time?"

He considers his options while chewing on his bottom lip. "Yeah, send her over Wednesday morning. I'll talk to her." He's being nice to me again.

When we finish, another hour later, he takes the garbage outside. I wash my hands, clean out the sink and wipe off the counter with lemon juice.

"Reach the big pot up there for me please sir."

He sets the pot on the kitchen island and pulls his stool over to watch. "Would I be going out on a limb here if I told you, I love your gray eyes?"

I give him a stern frown.

"I could lessen the romantic part by saying they match the color of the shrimp."

He dodges when I try to swat him.

"They have these little yellow speckles in them. Your eyes, not the shrimp."

"*Humph.*" I return to breaking up salad greens, slicing tomatoes, cucumbers, carrots and radishes. He drizzles on the salad dressing and pours two glasses of sweet tea. When the water boils, spicy herbs and shrimp slide in the pot.

5

The de-veined shrimp turn pink within seconds. They drain in my new stainless steel colander while we finish the salad.

I bought all new pots and pans after receiving a large inheritance from my Aunt Grace. My life began again when I bought and remodeled a coastal home. Now, I'm carefully getting all the things I've always wanted, including fixtures, stainless steel appliances, bright colored walls and my big kitchen sink.

We carry the spicy shrimp and salad-loaded plates with our glasses of ice tea out to the backyard. The warm southwest breeze, causing shimmers across the sound, catches up the ocean saltiness and tosses it across the banks into our faces. We eat in silence for a while, enjoying the view of sand bars and gnarled oak trees crouching near the water.

"What made you," he dips a big shrimp in ketchup, "decide to come back?"

"Morehead City is home." My heart swells. "Working with my hands and finishing a project is what I do best." My nail-nubs, calloused palms and incurably dry skin attest to my work history.

"I don't see how you managed. I mean, I know you used to help your daddy work on his boat and around the house, but frankly, back then, a girl couldn't get hired in construction." He wipes his mouth on the back of his wrist.

I hand him an extra paper towel I tucked in my pocket before I came out. "I was one of the first girls taking classes in electrical work at NC State. With my instructor's recommendation, the management company hired me. It was good training. Lord knows, this house was a mess when I bought it." I glance at the yellow vinyl-covered house and freshly painted back porch. "I did, however, forget if the fishing is good or surf is up, it's hard to get workers on the job around here."

He chuckles. "You can't teach the locals any different."

"Grace's home in New Bern is forty miles away and up the river. I wanted to come back to Morehead." I take another deep breath, inhaling the salt air. "Don't get me wrong. I loved her house. Even today, the smell of boxwoods reminds me of swinging on her front porch. "Christmas was the best. She flounced a big cedar tree in the front bay window, decorated with red bows, crystals and homemade ornaments." I sigh remembering the festivities. "I was blessed."

"I went there with you a couple of times." He encourages me. "We'd climb in a big magnolia tree in the front yard."

"They cut it down." A space balloons in my chest. "I rode by the last time I went through New Bern. The new owners chopped down most of the yard shrubbery, too. I can see Grace, hands on her hips, shaking her head, to think they would cut down all her trees." I wipe my eyes with a corner of my paper towel. "I loved visiting, but it wasn't here, in Morehead City. I wanted a place on the water, close to town. Grier and I visited a slew of houses before we found this one. This neighborhood suits me. It's lived in."

"Well, you certainly did a job on this old house," he says. "When you told me what you planned to do, I couldn't picture it. You turned it into a very attractive and I might add, comfortable home." He leans in close and grins. "We aren't exactly spring chickens anymore. I don't know where you found the energy."

I push him back. "I found it the same place you do when you're out on the water pulling in a full net or hauling books around in your store. We find it because we love it and don't start calling me an old woman. When was the last time you peeked in the mirror?"

"Ouch!" He ducks my verbal blow. "It is nice here." He kicks a bare foot out onto the back step and stretches.

In spite of myself, I soak up his kind words. "Thank you. You did all right, yourself. Who'd have thought our class valedictorian would own a bookstore, two fishing boats and play organ music on occasion?"

Danny shrugs off my comments. He graduated from Carolina and went off to a highfalutin' job out of state. I was interested in Matt back then and didn't pay Danny the attention he deserved. During the past months, I've managed to keep our conversations brief. My side-stepping around Danny is like walking barefoot among prickly blowfish.

Karen Dodd

I know little about his current personal life. Today, my curiosity gets the better of me. "Why'd you come back?"

"You remember my sister Nancy?"

His pale freckled-faced little sister with curly dark hair followed us around when we were younger, rarely saying a word.

"When she was diagnosed with cancer, she asked me to come back, help with her store and take her back and forth to the cancer treatment center. By the time she recovered, I enjoyed the bookstore and this leisure life too much to leave. She let me buy in. It suits us both. With my additional capital, we relocated and expanded the shop. I've been doing it for over fifteen years next autumn."

"You both still live in your mama and daddy's house?"

"Yes." He stares with both eyebrows raised, "You remember where it is?" probably surprised when I nod.

Chewing my last bite of shrimp, I remember the days we used to fish off his dock. The big white frame and fieldstone home is located at the edge of town. A long pier with a fishing boat tagged the shoreline behind the house. Now most of the pine tree forest is gone. Discount stores, restaurants and parking lots edge up to a slender barrier of trees.

"I added a den to the back of the house. Nancy and I rarely see each other when we're home, except when we're in the kitchen." He shifts in his chair, setting his plate on the back porch steps.

His face beams out pride when he talks about his family. "She grew up pretty, despite the fact she doesn't think so. It must be the cancer thing. Lately, Nancy wants me out of the house in the evenings. I think she's got a boyfriend, doesn't want me around when he calls."

"Sometimes a woman wants to be alone in a quiet house and to be surrounded by the things she loves. Don't misjudge her."

He flinches at my words. We carry the dishes back into the house. He grabs up his empty cooler.

I try not to wince when he gives me a peck on the cheek.

"I better go. Thanks for lunch." He looks at me as if he's going to say something but changes his mind.

"Thank you for my shrimp."

"Don't forget what I said about Mrs. Byrd. You take care of yourself, Quinn. I like having you around."

A train whistles in the distance, distracting us. The sound I enjoyed in the early mornings as a child now reminds me of a keening woman. I shiver as the sound melts into a moan. He raises an eyebrow, winks and heads for the front door. Mentioning all the accidental deaths among the elderly combined with the train wail prickles the hair on the back of my head.

TWO

The next morning, the dressing table mirror shows my love handles sagging over my waistband. I recall my wedding picture, a slender me in lace and white satin. Since my divorce, I have used my weight to shield myself from men. But loneliness has haunted me more years than I care to admit. A rogue wave swallowed Daddy and his fishing trawler right after I left Matt. Mama died the same day as Daddy, but it took a year for her body to quit living. I threw out the picture and my past when I left home following Mama's funeral. Aunt Grace wanted me to come live with her, but I stoned up my heart and headed for Raleigh.

My neighbor's door slams, breaking me away from those long ago images. My bedroom window looks out over his garden. He's going to his tool shed. He does it every morning.

The pre-set coffeemaker will blink on in thirty minutes. The warm spring air draws me outside for my T'ai Chi exercises. I step off the back porch and assume the first position. After three years of arm waving and waist twists, my body knows the routine. My mind focuses on breathing in concert with movement.

I enrolled in a T'ai Chi class in Raleigh years ago, because a resident of my building wanted someone to go with her. The teacher, a wrinkled Chinese man, in a blue frog-fastened jacket whirled his hands. He rarely spoke except to say, "Like this, try again, please." The entire class shifted bodies and moved arms until he was satisfied. My fingers and palms flushed red from working my chi. He told us, "Flexibility, balance and energy -- now again, please." The names of the moves fascinated me. Wave hands like clouds, carry tiger to the mountain, white cock stands on one leg. I learned the moves and became addicted to the exercise. My aching joints and vertigo improved. I graduated from his class, wearing my own baggy pants and blue frog-fastened jacket. The exercise became a part of my morning habit.

Begin Again, Quinn

Before breaking from the final stance, I take another series of slow breaths. The Chinese breathing technique forces me to relax and focus. It's both calming and invigorating.

I wouldn't be living on the coast if it hadn't been for Grace's generosity. I feel like she's been watching over me these past few months.

A Bible verse flashes into my mind. "May the Lord watch between me and thee, while we are absent one from the other." My mama drilled Bible verses into my head when I was a child and they often float to the surface.

Colorful irises spike in the garden. They replace the earlier blooming tulips and daffodils. A fountain bubbles over stones and washes into a small pond. A cardinal pecks at the feeder and calls his mate. Scanning Bogue Sound, I watch sea gulls rise above a barge-pushing tug.

The narrow band of land running east to west along the North Carolina coast joins the north-south leg of the Outer Banks with the better known islands of Ocracoke, Bodie and Hatteras. Each fall, boating snowbirds travel along this sound to their Florida docksides or islands of the Caribbean. Every spring, the live-aboards, in their trawlers and sailboats, plow their way north along the same waters of the Intracoastal Waterway.

I watch two north-bound sailboats meet and glide past the barge. Having grown up on the waterfront, a whiff of salt marsh is better than a jolt of coffee to wake me. I missed this when I lived in Raleigh.

Wiping a handful of dirt from the back steps, I recall my father's long fingers looked a lot like mine. Daddy always said, "If something's worth doing, it's worth doing right the first time." While I worked on this old house, I felt my daddy watching and telling me, "You done good, Shug."

My sock-covered feet find their way into worn clogs as I lift the recycle bin through the backdoor. The coffee's brewing and the aroma leads me through the hall to the front door as the coffee maker gives its last bubbly whoosh. Pushing open the front screen door with my hip, I bang my crate of cans, bottles and paper to the curb. Weekly offerings to the recycling gods call for a sacrifice before seven o'clock. I forgot to put it out last night.

Pulling the paper from its box, I watch Charles Goodwin crouch in his garden, tugging weeds and flailing at gnats.

My telephone kept shutting off during my refurbishing. It was something about the lines with all the digging and rewiring. Charles offered the use of his phone. A slim man with sparse hair and few words, he provided a chair in his kitchen while my fingers did the walking through his yellow pages. "Ah, it's you. Want to use the phone, I suppose. Here, sit and take your time. I'll be in the yard." My new neighbor hustled out of his house as I made calls to suppliers, repairmen and utility companies.

Towards the end of construction, if he saw me coming, he opened the door and allowed me passage. He tolerated my presence with a few grunts and murmurs. "They didn't fix it yet? Strange, they can't find your problem." He mumbled as he disappeared out the door.

"*Helloooo*, Charles." I wave at him.

Every morning, he's chopping or poking in the ground, more like a drill sergeant than a colonel, prodding his rows of green into formation.

Grier told me, "Charles is a Marine. Once a Marine, always a Marine," she winked, "and a widower." Grier married a Marine after graduating from college and speaks from experience.

"How are you today?" I bet it irritates Charles, but he straightens to answer me.

He pulls himself up, tugs at his floppy hat and salutes me, "Morning Ms. Winslow. I'm fine. Thanks for asking."

"Now Charles, I told you to call me Quinn. We're neighbors. It's okay to use first names." I stroll up my walk, banging the paper on my leg as I go. "Sorry to disturb you."

He grunts, assuming parade rest. When he's satisfied I have nothing more to say, he bends to pick up his tools and weed bucket. "Damn!" He holds his back as he carefully moves to his workshop behind the garden. He seems to favor his back a lot when I'm around.

Begin Again, Quinn

On the front porch, I set my coffee aside, pull out a chair and spread the paper on a wicker table I brought from Grace's house. Since the weather warmed, the front porch is a favorite perch for my paper browsing and the crossword puzzle. I read the obituaries first. I know more people listed there than I find on the front page.

"Rose Issen Dies

Rose Issen, 91, of Arapahoe died in her home on Monday evening. A native of Pamlico County, she is survived by a sister, Meredith Holmes of Clearwater, Florida. It is believed carbon monoxide poisoning from a malfunctioning heater caused her death.

She was a quilter with the local Smooth Waters Quilting Association. Services will be at the Fishermen of the Sea Chapel in Arapahoe on Saturday at three o'clock."

Danny will argue the Little-Old-Lady-Murderer has struck again. This news item piques my interest. After all, I'm a member of this elite group of single elders. If there's someone targeting old folks, I need to know about it. I tear out the notice after checking to see if there's anything noteworthy on the backside. I'll start a collection, morbid as it sounds. There can't be as many deadly accidents as Danny claims.

After reading the death notices, I turn to the comics. The phone rings and I scuttle inside to answer it.

Grier greets me and says, "I'm walking my dog at the beach today. Want to come?" She's always multi-tasking. I hear water running, probably from her breakfast dishes and her television blares in the background. Without waiting for my response, she says, "We can walk every day if you want."

Our mothers were sisters. We were named after two great-aunts. She went off to college and became a teacher. I married Matt after graduating from high school. Unlike mine, her marriage was one of those happily-ever-after ones. With my inheritance, I'm enchanted, a bit like Cinderella, but without the prince. I prefer prince-less.

I am Grier's new project, like when we were younger. She styled my hair or showed me how to accent my positives.

I laugh into the phone and say, "I know what you're up to. I appreciate it. Sure, walking sounds good. I was String Bean in grade school. Now I look more like a lima!"

"Quinn," she whines, "you always belittle yourself. I remember the trim attractive girl you used to be."

"She is a large woman now." I pinch the roll of flesh between two fingers that makes me feel like the Michelin Woman. "With all the remodeling I did, I thought I'd lose some poundage."

"I believe you'll drop the weight when you change the way you think about yourself, young lady."

"Is this your guidance counselor voice speaking?" I know she's right.

Ever since she saw the movie, *Gone With The Wind*, Grier exaggerates her Southern accent. "May as well use some of my education. Teaching and being a guidance counselor provided me with a tolerance, accepting things that won't change but you need change." She pauses giving me a chance to wipe the ugly Matthew memories out of my mind. "We're going to work on your attitude, also, Cousin." In the background, her television goes silent. "I'll be there in fifteen minutes, honey."

"I'll be ready." I munch on a Danish pastry from the bakery six-pack hidden in the refrigerator, rinse out the coffee pot and dash to the bathroom. While digging in the closet for my wide-brimmed hat, I hear her car beep.

Grier drives a twelve-year old red Volvo station wagon. She hauled her sons and their friends to soccer camp and ballgames in the very same car. I never know what I'll find in the front seat. She brushes McDonald's wrappers to the floor as I open the passenger door.

I fasten my seatbelt and sit back, clutching my hat. My feet nestle in a bed of fast food foil and cardboard wrappers. "Tell me how you eat that stuff and not gain an ounce."

She pulls out of my neighborhood, driving like Richard Petty, zigzagging through traffic, forgetting to use turn signals and speeding when she shouldn't.

"I don't know. I think at this stage, I'm immune to it. Quinn," she reaches over and pats my thigh. "I haven't mentioned this in the past few months but I felt awful about not looking you up when Sam transferred back here. I didn't know how to find you." Grier apologizes. Her husband went back to school and now works as a police detective.

"No matter, I'm back," I say. "The thing about a true friend is you can slide right back into a comfortable relationship, like a pair of favorite old shoes."

"I like it. We're a pair of mildewed Weejens under the bed." She chuckles. Her short dark hair dances in the breeze from the rolled-down window. Large tortoise-shell sunglasses hide her eyes. She's wearing a skin tight long sleeved purple shirt and running shorts. She's been racing from one place to another all her life. I think she even jogs in place while waiting in the grocery line.

I pull my big shirt over my stretch pants as she cuts off a little sports car. "Only good luck and reciprocal relations with law enforcement agencies keep you from collecting speeding tickets." I joke about her driving.

"No tickets in twenty-five years, so you must be right," she grins. Crinkles around her eyes and mouth betray years of working in her yard and sitting at ballgames without a hat. I wish I had her confidence. She jokes about still being able to wear her wedding dress. I share those same skinny genes. Now all I have to do is rediscover mine.

She breaks me out of my pity pot. "Don't be so glum. Give me a positive greeting." She beams at me.

I feel smug as I smooth down my shirt. "The remodeling is officially finished. I do appreciate you getting me out of the house and starting a serious exercise program."

"You're welcome." Always a toucher, she reaches over to squeeze my hand.

The big Akita in the back of the Volvo stands as we drive over the high-rise bridge. He slobbers on my shoulder. I reach back, scratch his broad head and rub his drool off my hand onto my pants.

Grier scolds him. "Mojo, no. Lie back down. We'll be there in a minute." Then she turns to me, "I'm sorry. I thought he'd behave himself until we got to the beach. I didn't walk him much this morning, just enough to do his business before we came."

"No problem."

Loosening the white-knuckle grip on my hat, I enjoy the view from the high-rise bridge. Hotel rooftops simmer in the western part of the island. I nod to the Atlantic Ocean on the horizon outlining houses. "They haven't built tall enough yet to block the ocean view. Remember when the Ferris wheel and carousel lit up the night."

Grier's eyes aren't on the road. Her gaze follows her hands as she waves them at both sides of the causeway. "Beach towel places, condominiums, bathing suit shops and party boat fishing centers. Welcome to the beach. They're going to tear down the camp grounds and a mobile home park to put up more condominiums and palm trees, for heavens sakes. If God had wanted palm trees on this island, he'd have left off all the pines, water oaks and cedar trees. Pretty soon you won't be able to tell us from Myrtle Beach!" She shakes her head as she pulls into a beachside parking space.

I stretch my arms and legs while she leashes her giant dog. Trying to get my bearings I say, "The Pavilion used to be here, didn't it?"

The temple of beach music attracted teenagers like moths to a street light. Young Marines from the nearby bases and college students crowded into the wooden framed building listening to the Embers and the Band of Oz. The smells of beer and popcorn seeped into the night air.

She responds, "Yep, our loss. They sold pieces of the building to Pavilion worshipers. The town beautification committee took the money and built this brick walkway to the beach."

We leave our shoes in the car and walk the warm surface. Each brick bears the initials or names of contributors. Like the yellow brick road, the bricks lead the way to beach lover's Oz, the sand and ocean. The ocean's saltiness flavors the air.

Grier hands me a pair of scrunched up grocery sacks. "I want you to get some shells for the bowl I gave you as a house-warming gift. An empty bowl collects nothing but dust. We may as well pick up trash, too."

Begin Again, Quinn

We slog through the sand, out towards the surf and stoop to examine the sand. Cigarette butts mix with shell treasures, tiny coquinas and part of an olive shell.

"Remember when we could find whole sand dollars and cockle shells?" I rinse the shells off in the cool water. Each successive wave sucks my feet deeper into the sand.

At this hour, gulls pick at the froth along the water's edge. The dog chases ghost crabs along the foam as Grier expands and then contracts the leash when another beach walker approaches.

"So what's new with your neighbor?" She smiles, bending to pick up a beer bottle. "Or are you still letting Danny court you?"

"Danny's just a friend." I mirror her, squatting to pick up a plastic bag and cup from the surf. "Don't waste time playing Dr. Love on my account. Charles doesn't give me a second thought."

"Hon, believe me. He notices you. Don't you have any little urges drawing you to either of those two available men?"

"I'm not feeling any urges, other than indigestion." I begin to squirm.

"It'll be a crime if you don't fix yourself up and send out a few flirtations. You have a lot to offer, my dear lady."

I kick a spray of water into the air. "I don't want a man in my life." There, I said it.

"You think you don't. You've never had a good man." She gives me one of her irritated teacher frowns, with her hands on her hips. "I know Charles is watching you. You're within," she makes rabbit ears with her fingers, "'his perimeter of surveillance.' Why don't we go to my favorite boutique in New Bern? You can afford to buy new clothes now, Quinn. You need a decent haircut, too." She drops her bag to the sand, wipes her hands on her pants and pulls at my hair. She's trying to find a L'Oreal moment. "We'll get you a Clinique make-over, too. Nothing extreme, just accent your positives. With those big gray eyes of yours, you need to wear more purple."

"Danny thinks my eyes are the same color as fresh shrimp," I enlighten her.

"He's such a romantic." She clutches her hands under her chin and flashes me several hairy eyeballs.

I laugh and push my cheeks in with my fingers to feel the cheekbones she envisions. In spite of myself, I smile. "Did you get another woman's romance magazine? Honestly, I have too many things going on to think about sprucing up or flirting. I have my church activities and Help & Hands, now the walking and a stack of mystery books to read and get back to you."

Grier stops to untangle the dog from a lifeguard's empty stand. "You don't do anything for yourself, Quinn. You deserve a little fun. Lord knows you deserve a good man in your life."

"Men don't go searching for someone like me, especially Charles. I never could flirt. I know for a fact Danny is letting his memory corrupt his current perception. He likes me because of our history together. I'm not fooled by his wooing."

"You have thought this whole man thing out," she grins.

I grimace.

"Okay, okay, no more about the men in your life," she says. "Look at this beach. Can you believe the trash they leave?"

"Ouch! It hurts too." I brush a shell off my foot, noting our footprints up to this point reflect Grier's light-hearted gait and my solid steps. Mojo's paw prints scatter wet sand between them.

"You were always a tenderfoot. You know it's about prom time. We used to be getting a tan. Look at us now, walking this beach with big hats, fanny packs and scooping poop."

Begin Again, Quinn

She glances up the beach. "There's Eleanor Aldridge. Heavens, the water's so rough today. How can she swim in it? Hello, Eleanor!"

As Grier and I quicken our pace, a lean swimmer leaves the surf and walks toward us.

"Good morning, I see I'm not the only little old lady hitting the beach this morning. It's going to be a nice day, don't you think?" The newcomer speaks with a mid-western accent. Dark blue eyes study me from beneath her wet locks. The classic navy swimsuit outlines her slender figure.

"Yes, it does. Listen, I wanted to get y'all together. This is my cousin, Quinn Winslow. Quinn, this is Eleanor Aldridge. She's president of my Golden Girls' Investment Club."

Eleanor gives me a shrewd looking over while she shakes my hand.

Grier continues to address me, "Since you're through with your remodeling, you need to join our club."

I discourage the idea. "Oh, I know squat about investments. Everything's with the bank. I'm a safe depositor."

Eleanor places a cool hand on my sun-warmed wrist. "Well, we do have a vacancy in the group since Margaret Byrd died. Poor thing, her husband died, what, two years ago? She'd begun to get out; told me she met someone nice." She winks. "We even went shopping for new clothes and makeup the day she died. What a terrible accident." She lifts her shoulders in despair. "She said it was getting serious. But…" She swallows and shakes her head. "Why don't you come to a couple of meetings?" Eleanor's skin goose bumps in the breeze. "Brr, my condo's just up the beach. Can you come up for a cup of coffee?" She runs her hands along her arms for warmth.

"Not today, this four-legged beast wants to go and we have errands." Grier yanks him back.

"I'll be seventy-two this September and I never miss my morning swim in the surf. Leaving the water gives me the shivers." She reaches over to pet Mojo. "My son says it's foolish for me to swim in the ocean. He's afraid I'll drown." Eleanor shades her face and scans the horizon. "Some say drowning isn't a bad way to go. One intake and it's over. *Ha.*" She gives a quick laugh to emphasize her remark.

"Hush, please don't say anything about your druthers for dying!" Grier flutters her hands at Eleanor.

"Well, accidents happen. You never know when your time will come," she says.

I've just met the woman and she makes a remark echoing Danny's suspicion. "Can we take a rain check?"

"Sure, I'll catch you another day." Eleanor jogs up to her boardwalk. We wave hurried goodbyes.

The dog pulls away, heading after a flock of shore birds. My mind returns to Eleanor's remark about death -- by accidental drowning.

THREE

Eleanor disappears over the dunes as we continue our beach walk. The smell of salt air and seagulls screaming overhead allows me a moment of solace before Grier brings up the question of joining the investment club again.

"You really need to get out more and meet people. Joining the group will give you a chance to meet ladies like yourself." Grier isn't giving up. "You know, single, survivors, with a bit of money to jingle in the pockets."

"She seems like a nice lady." I hesitate. "But I don't know about joining an investment club. Aren't stocks risky?"

"I wouldn't introduce you unless I thought you could handle it. Besides, it's not investing everything with us. Each member puts in a thousand dollars yearly."

"Wow! A thousand dollars used to be a lot of money for me. Now, I pull about that amount off my own investments monthly to cover expenses."

An angler on the distant pier pulls at his tugging rod. His fishing leads wink in the sunlight.

Grier continues, "I go on-line to do research. We're not trying to make a killing in the market. We're careful."

I fend off again, "I don't know anything about investments. I don't even own a computer."

"You can use mine or go to the library and use theirs. Eleanor keeps the computer program with our monthly progress reports. Some members ante-up more money and increase their gains -- or losses. Eleanor is the only one who knows how much each of us puts in and what it's worth now."

We continue walking toward the fishing pier.

"The few basics you need to learn about investing, I'll teach you." She's back in her classroom as she starts counting on her fingers. "Like one, pay yourself first. If you get any new money from stock gains, presents, loan payoffs, then you invest half of it."

"Grace used to do that. Each month she put money in savings and she lived off what she had left. I guess it's like my pickle jar where I dump all my loose change. When it's full I buy myself clothes at the consignment store." I grin. "Second-hand clothiers provide all my clothes." I make a gentle curtsy and pull my shorts out at the sides, like a gown.

"Hmm, we'll see about your wardrobe, but you got the savings part right."

"At this point in my life I'm doing more spending than saving. Finishing the house took a hunk."

I remember Grace's attorney at the probate meeting. He wore a bow tie and tweed jacket, drawling his concerns to me with his careful Southern dialect. The first check he gave me, even before he sold Grace's house, was enough to buy my new home and pay for all the renovations. I was flabbergasted. "I'll need a new car one of these days."

"You *are* familiar with investment basics." Grier holds up two fingers. "Adequate cash reserves. You know, like your money markets, certificates of deposit, checking and savings account. If you need a new car or an emergency comes up, you don't have to sell your stock at a loss if the market is down. Sam and I keep three to four month's worth of living expenses in the credit union."

She holds up a third finger. "Balance and diversify your money."

"Don't put all your eggs in one basket," I agree.

"Right, spread it out."

I begin to fidget. Grier's overloading me.

"Our club members help each other. It's comforting to know if something happened to Sam, God forbid, I'd have someone to talk with about finances.

"The only unique thing about our investment club is the survivor-right's clause. We agreed if one of us should die the rest split her share equally."

"That's different!" From the shade of the fishing pier, I squint into the sunlight. The sun spatters through the overhead boardwalk making shadows, like piano keys on the sand. "I've never heard of any group doing that."

Grier shrugs, "We had no idea the clause would function so soon. Then Margaret died. At first, I was uncomfortable dividing her portion, but we all agreed. The strength of the members built the investment pool." Pulling a pad of lip-gloss from her waist pouch, she applies a dab to her mouth. "I know Birdie wanted us to do it."

The dog sniffs at the creosote-coated pilings supporting the overhead pier. Dirty foam from the waves undulates in each slap of the surf. The smell of dead fish and old beer sours the air.

She continues, "The market is crazy these days, so we decided to meet briefly mid-month too." The lip gloss drops back into her pouch. "I think we have over a quarter-million dollars in our pool."

"Lord have mercy. What a lot of money," I exclaim.

"With Birdie gone, there are nine of us in the club."

I'm still hedging. "I'll try to make the next meeting. I'm not making any promises." I toss my bag of trash into a garbage can chained to the pier pilings. "Before Grace's death, I never had any money. She did invest in the market."

"See, it's not dangerous with good research," she says.

"The Bible says we should be good stewards. I'm acting like the steward who buried his talents in the ground. I promise to think about it."

Rose Issen's obituary, snipped from the paper, slides into a plastic sleeve in a three-ring binder. He keeps a record of all his victims -- his special clients. Orchestrating deadly accidents is good for business, very profitable. The notebook snaps shut.

People enjoy knowing they are one of a select group. Miss Issen jumped at his offer. Her big home overlooks the Neuse River and is a prime piece of real estate with acreage.

Rose lived comfortably on a civil service pension. She never married. Most of her lifelong friends died years before. Winter drafts found their way through window frames and underneath doorsills. She didn't want to heat the whole house. She purchased the space heater the previous winter.

She also used it when the cool spring nights left her house damp and chilly. Before going to bed Monday night Rose made a note. She wanted to call the heating people who sent out that nice young person to check her kerosene heater. A money-

23

pincher, Rose hadn't called for the service. It was unfortunate Rose Issen never installed carbon monoxide detectors in her home.

FOUR

"Charles," I call to him after walking out to get my morning newspaper. "Do you know anything about investment clubs?" I lean over his picket fence and wave my Saturday paper.

Charles stands up, straight posture casting a shadow in the morning sun. He removes his hat and squints, "I know if you don't know what you're doing you better not belong. Be careful, understand?" He walks towards me. "There's a couple of clubs I know about in town, mainly high finance. Why?"

"I was invited to join a ladies' investment club. Someone told me I need my money to be working harder. What do you think? You used to work in investments, didn't you?"

He waves his hand, as if he's shooing a fly. "Yes, when I retired from the Marine Corps I worked as an investment advisor. Never put anything in the market you can't afford to live without, for a while at least and some people lose it forever. Here, give me that." He grabs my newspaper and reaches for his ever-present ballpoint pen clipped in his shirt pocket.

He writes two book titles in the margin, a woman's name and telephone number. Talking like a machine gun, he rattles on. "These are basic investment books. Get them from the library. I used to work with this woman. Most of my clients went over to her when I retired. Make an appointment. Forget about investment clubs." He tips his hat, does a quick turn and walks to his work shed, toting his hoe on his shoulder, as if he were carrying an old carbine.

Deciphering Charles' scribbling, I return to my house. On Monday, I'll call and make an appointment.

The phone rings. I tuck it between my chin and shoulder as I rinse out my morning dishes.

"Hello, Quinn, how are you these days?" Matt's voice hasn't changed in forty years.

It feels like a cold spike tapping into the top of my spine. My coffee cup shatters on the floor. I nearly drop the receiver.

"I understand you are doing quite well. I deserve to share in some of the cash you've been slopping out all over town. A couple of thousand should do to start, should I come by or do you want to mail me a check?"

My hand grips the sink's edge. For a split second, I am a young woman ducking his fists, cringing in the corner. "You, you needn't come by here and I'm not sending any money." My voice sounds stronger than I feel.

"Playing it cool, are you? You remember how I used to rob your pickle jar. It sounds to me like you got yourself a pickle barrel now. *Ha, ha.*" His hyena laugh snaps my head back as if he had hit me. "There's ways to get money out of you. I learned. You got rid of my last name, but you're not rid of me, Miss Quinn Winslow. I'll see you around." He disconnects.

I would have reacted differently years ago, but working at the Domestic Abuse Center, I've learned to accept my past. My problem was not leaving him sooner. I bend to pick up the broken pieces of my cup. By the time the china chip clinks into the trashcan, I feel like I shoveled away road-kill. Amazed my hands aren't shaking and my breath is normal, I mumble a prayer of gratitude.

It's better to think of something else. Reaching for my morning paper with Charles' scribbles, I decide to visit the library. I take a quick shower and pull on my best pair of consignment rack slacks.

The county library is located in Beaufort, across the Newport River east of Morehead City. As I drive over the bridge, new construction glares at me. Radio Island was once beaches, a fishing pier and a place we anchored for family picnics. I scowl at the commercial business and condominiums gobbling up the remaining shoreline.

Begin Again, Quinn

As a girl, I rode my bicycle to the old converted railroad station/library. Today, a brick-faced structure replaces the creaky wooden-floored building. Wedged between a row of cedars and the historically recognized Masonic Lodge, a parking lot offers a shady spot to park.

I push the glass door inward, expecting old book and waxed floor odors. Instead, the smell of plastic chairs and new carpeting attacks my nose and a security bell dings my entrance. Fingering through a side display of brochures, I pull out a couple, then approach the front desk.

"I'm new in the area. I'd like to get a library card and find out what's available." I greet the attendant with a smile.

The pale woman peers over her glasses and slaps forms down on the counter. She pulls a sharpened pencil from a desk drawer. Her monotone voice drones, "I need to see your driver's license to verify residence."

She studies my picture and blows her nose on a tissue before handing me back my identification. "Fill this out. A four-year card is ten dollars, there's an additional fee if you want to use the Internet. Read this," she hands me a bright pink card, "and take the library self-guided tour. If you need assistance, we're here to help." The tight-smiled woman takes my money and returns to her filing.

I wander through the paperback exchange, reference section and copying facilities, stopping at a computer carrel. A woman scrolls down a page clicking a gadget with her finger and making notes in a spiral notebook.

"You look like you know what you're doing. I'm envious." I venture when she stops and smiles up at me.

"Is this your first time here? I can tell by the look on your face you don't know beans about the Internet. I don't mind sharing. Pull up a chair." The computer wizard winks at me. The glare of the screen reflects in her large bifocals. From her glasses, a colorful loop of beaded chain dangles down and around her neck. A multicolored sweater matches her green blouse and slacks.

She waits while I drag a chair beside her. "I'm Katherine Knowles. Are you new in town or just visiting?"

"Yes, no, well, I lived here a long time ago. Quinn Winslow. Nice to meet you."

We shake hands. Katherine looks straight into my eyes, not giving my consignment store clothes a second glance.

"I've moved back a few months ago." I nod toward the computer screen. "Never used one of those things, much less the Internet. Is it hard to learn?"

Katherine rolls her chair forward and moves her clicker. Her arthritic-gnarled fingers stumble along the keys. "No, it's not hard. Watch. I wouldn't be here, but mine's out while they upgrade the memory." She sees the scrap of paper in my hand. "You have some books you're looking for?"

She takes my note, maneuvering through the electronic card catalog and finds both of Charles' books. She writes the numbers on the paper stub. "There you go." The screen changes and a colorful display pops up. "We'll have some fun, now."

She explains computer terms, how to use an Internet server and find my way around. Every time her head moves, the beaded eyeglass chain swings at her cheek. "It's easy," she says.

"It doesn't look easy to me."

"I'm looking up stock for my post-menopausal women's investment club." She chuckles under her breath. "That's what my nephew calls it. We're all of a certain age, if you know what I mean." She taps her temple. "The club keeps the old brain working. I can only play so much bridge and golf. I wanted something I can mull over, make choices and live with the consequences."

"Do you belong to the same club as Grier Dew and Eleanor Aldridge?" I ask. "Grier's my cousin."

Begin Again, Quinn

"So, you're related to Grier. I believe she mentioned you." She nods at me, her eyebrows forming crescents over her glasses.

"They want me to come to the next meeting. I just met Eleanor."

"I'd like for you to join." Her eyes narrow as she hunches over to reveal a secret. "I knew squat about investments when we started, so I had a system. See, my last name is Knowles. Maiden name was Kelson. All my initials are k's. In the beginning, I only looked up companies starting with a K. It narrows the field for what's available. I've branched out now since getting the hang of the basics, but I still go back to the k's."

She sits back in her chair. "I have to say we certainly did well with Krispy Kreme. It tripled and split twice after we bought it. We sold it off before the last big dive. Right now, it's down because of all the low-carbohydrate diet commotion and bad business decisions, but I still think it's one to own."

"Is that right?" My mouth waters. "I'm very familiar with Krispy Kreme on the consumer end."

"Now there's something to remember. Invest in a company you'd buy from." She continues to educate me. "When they started putting doughnuts in the fast-gas places, the quality dropped. Who wants to buy Krispy Kremes after you pump gas? The flavor's not the same. In grocery stores, they taste a day old. I quit buying them there, but if I go to Greenville or Goldsboro, I'll drive by where they make them to get me a couple of hot ones with a cup of coffee."

"I never ate a hot Krispy Kreme doughnut."

She places a pudgy hand over her heart, "They're to die for! If Krispy Kreme stuck to their individual stores with hot fresh doughnuts, they wouldn't be in this financial mess. People don't give up their Krispy Kreme doughnuts." She licks her top lip. "I certainly haven't. Well, let me get back to encouraging you to join our group. We all recommend interesting stocks to buy. Of course, I've recommended some dud companies, too. But that's the fun of a club. We have to agree on each purchase or sale." She pauses. "I think our club's return beats most portfolios. It's a known fact women's investment clubs do better than others."

"Really?" The Club is sounding better to me all the time.

Katherine rolls her mouse around a listing of her "k" investments. "Hmm, let's see, KBM. There's a new one. Let's look it up." While she waits for the screen to change, Katherine sucks in her bottom lip. "This is interesting. It's located right here in North Carolina, with a Raleigh address. They buy up old life insurance policies. These underlined phrases link to other sites, see?" She clicks back and forth so I understand.

I nod my head staring at the blank-filled screen, not knowing enough to comment.

"Back here, see, they offer a very good percentage of your death benefit for their purchase of your old life insurance policies. I might be interested. I have no children or husband. Let me type my name and address in this space and see what I get back." She folds her hands primly across her lap. "See, it's easy and fun. Have anything you want to research?"

"Humph, I don't know enough to ask a question. I'm sure you have better things to do than tutor me on the computer." I stand, returning my chair to the other table. "Sorry to take up so much of your time." I gather my purse and note from Charles. "Thanks for sharing. I have to admit, it doesn't look as scary now. Thank you, Katherine."

"Call me Kat, all my friends do. Don't run off. I'll be through in a few minutes. Want to see the sights on the waterfront and have lunch?"

"Sure. I'll find my books and meet you at the entrance." I smile. "It's hard for me to believe I'm really retired and have nowhere I must go."

Begin Again, Quinn

Ten minutes later, we drive the three blocks down to the waterfront and park our separate cars in the free parking area. Unusual gift shops and chandleries line both sides of the street along with a variety of restaurants. We browse through the local stores.

Beaufort, NC is a small town, founded in the early eighteenth century. For the past two centuries, pirates, privateers, Union forces and now boat cruisers and tourists invade it. Oleander, crepe myrtles and moss-draped oaks shade the sidewalks. The aroma of Cajun spices from waterfront restaurants lingers in the air. Unlike Beaufort, SC, where "Beau" sounds like two, the NC version "Beau-" rhymes with toe.

"I can tell you're going to fit right in our club." Kat leans toward me after checking over her shoulder. "Just between you and me, one of the members is a bit worrisome. Don't let her remarks worry you."

"I try not to let other people bother me anymore, but thanks for the warning." I stop to read a posted menu in a window. "Maybe I'll take a class on computers at the community college."

Kat bobs her head. "I did, but using one is really how you learn." She draws herself up and takes a deep breath. "I've lived here over twenty years and I never stop learning -- people, places, things." Her stomach growls. "Excuse me. Where do you want to eat?"

The posted Whaler's menu offers a tempting seafood gumbo. We push open the heavy door and walk to the hostess stand. She seats us by a window. Beyond the creek and islands, we can see the inlet to the Atlantic Ocean.

As we order, Katherine asks, "It doesn't have any clams in it, does it? I'm allergic to them. I don't even order fried food where they cook a bunch of seafood in the same oil. You know, maybe I'll stick to the broccoli and cheddar chowder."

When the waiter moves away, Kat pats her purse. "My friends know I keep an Epipen in my pocketbook. My doctor makes me carry them in case I ever have another reaction. I ended up in the hospital the last time I got a bit of clam. Heavens, they could kill me. You see, since moving down, I've learned to love grits. One of the restaurants fixes a brunch on Sundays. Of all things, the cook mixes grits with cream and clam juice. Well, I had no idea. I was getting up to fill my coffee when I toppled over. I was so embarrassed."

She turns to look at the water. Sail boats and power boats glide by from all over the world. Their colorful ensigns declare their port of origin.

Kat continues telling me about how she ended up on the coast. "I didn't mind my husband's transfer south. The winters are better than Minneapolis. I took up golf, sing in the church choir and am active in several volunteer groups."

As she talks, I imagine she's never met a stranger.

"My husband, Tom, always said if I went into the grocery store in a new town, I'd make a dozen friends before I got to the checkout." She stops and takes a tissue from her purse and wipes her eyes. "Tom died a few years back -- heart disease. I sat by his bedside. The monitors blinked a straight line and a nurse finally led me away." She stuffs her tissue in her pocket. "Good heavens, I've babbled on, haven't I?"

I change the subject by telling her about my move and home remodeling. "My aunt taught school in New Bern for thirty-three years. I had no idea she made me her heir. I'd thought I'd have to work the rest of my life."

"Imagine that. I'm so glad you spoke to me this morning. You'll enjoy meeting the others in our group. You'll fit right in. You're feisty, like the rest of us. There isn't much slowing us down these days." Her eyeglass chain waggles as her head nods.

When we part company, I sit in my car, windows down to let the breeze cool the car's interior. Boats and people parade by the waterfront, giving it a festive air. A double-tiered bus rolls by. When a megaphone voice reaches my ear, I catch snippets about Blackbeard and the offshore recovery of Queen Anne's Revenge.

Shifting gears, I back out of the parking space. Grier invited me to Sunday lunch while we were walking. She asked me to bring dessert.

At home, I thumb through my recipe box. Mama's smudged handwriting beckons as I finger through recollections as well as the recipes. I'm looking for my grandmother's orange cake recipe. I may as well make two. In for a penny, in for a pound. I pat my hips.

While the sugar and eggs cream in the mixer, I grate orange peel, break the nuts and measure dates. The fragrance of grated orange brings me back to my grandmother's side. As I continue baking, I'm a carefree girl again working beside my mother and grandmother in the kitchen.

FIVE

"But, I gained a pound after all those miles we walked this past week." A busy morning at church and the invitation to lunch brings me to Grier's home.

"Not to worry," Grier informs me. "Sweet heart, the exercise is replacing fat with muscle. Muscle weighs more."

"Piffle." I snort. "I'll admit my clothes feel a bit looser."

"Here, have a glass of tea and relax until the children get here. I know they'll be late. The little ones always make them run behind." She sits me at the kitchen counter and fills a tall glass with ice cubes.

"The grill's lit. I'll put the chicken on in a few minutes." Sam comes in the kitchen door. "Where's the drinks?" He begins to build a platter of marinated meat for the grill. Grier and I carry out a cooler of soft drinks.

I plop down on the chaise lounge, where I remain most of the afternoon. A car door slams and Grier and her husband welcome their family. Grier introduces me and I blend into the family picnic.

"Jason, honey, be careful. Don't ride your car too close to the edge." His mother, Julia, pulls a chair over to the gap at the porch steps. Her high pitched voice adds flavor to the gathering. She talks with a Carolina down-east brogue, making one-syllable words into two and straining her vowels. Most of the people living in this area used to speak with that accent.

Her child cycles around and around, never tiring of his race track. He finally dispatches the vehicle to find his way into my lap. The boy immediately kisses my cheek and clutches my neck with sticky hands. I'm surprised at the affection.

Begin Again, Quinn

"I love you, Aunt Quinn." It's what I think he says. His soft cheek brushes my own, creating an unfamiliar tingle in my chest.

I return a kiss to the top of his head inhaling his smell. "I love you too, Jason."

His short hair curls in dampness from his exertions. When he becomes bored with his perch, he climbs down to find another. His younger brother wobbles in a wind-up swing beside his mother.

I pull myself out of my lounge chair long enough to fill a plate and get a refill of the unsweetened tea. "Grier tells me you're expecting, Carolyn." I edge into the conversation.

"Yes, Daddy says to make it before the end of the year if we want a tax break." She laughs. "Only an accountant daddy would mention it, before he asks if it's a boy or girl." She leans towards me. "I'm hoping for a girl." She looks up at her husband as he approaches.

"Can I get you anything?" he asks.

"I'm fine. Ask your mama what she used to marinate this chicken. It's delicious."

Grier brings out my cake. She slices it and brings me a small piece. "Don't get up. You look comfortable. Let me take your dinner plate so you can handle this."

"Thank you. I feel like Queen for a Day. You're not letting me do much."

"Not much to do, yet. I'll recruit you later when they all leave." She sashays back over to play with a grandchild.

After the meal, the children begin to fuss. Sam, Jr. stands. He and Julia collect their kid gear. "Mama, everything was delicious. We need to get home." To his son he says, "You get fussy when it's naptime, don't you?" He shoulders his whining child. "Quinn, it was good to see you again." Sam, Jr. plumbed the new fixtures in my house and put in the water line for the back yard fountain.

"The pleasure is mine, Sam. I enjoyed sharing your children."

"Have you got your house finished? I like that fountain." He turns to his wife. "Julia, when these guys get older, we may replace the swing set with what she did in her back yard."

His wife clips the infant into the carrier. "We've got a ways to go, don't you think?" Julia puts a knapsack on his other shoulder, lifts her baby in his carrier and then gathers soft toys with her free hand. "Grier, Sam, thanks. Home cooking's always a treat for us. I hardly have time to cook these days with work and these two. Quinn, I enjoyed meeting you."

Grier's younger son and his wife Carolyn prepare to leave. Carolyn says, "Assure me this morning sickness it's worth the misery." She grins, holding her stomach, while her husband tugs her up.

Grier gives her a hug of support. As her sons and their families leave, Grier's eyes mist. Sam straightens up the deck and packs away chairs. I wait until he looks up.

"Sam," my hesitation gets his attention. "My former husband, Matt, called me on the phone the other day and tried to get me to pay him money so he'd stay away."

Sam, no longer the husband and father - but the police detective, leads me inside to sit down.

"I'm open to suggestions. He hasn't physically hurt me, yet."

Grier comes into the room. "What? Matt's called you after all these years?"

"He somehow knows I inherited money." I bite my top lip.

"Well Quinn, he beat you back then! You can't ignore his threat."

Begin Again, Quinn

"Daddy told us to work it out. Matthew would apologize and be sorry afterwards, but soon he went back to his old ways. Back then, you didn't get a divorce. You never heard of spouse abuse." My shoulders slump. "Being in love and married didn't crack up to all it was supposed to be. I still carry that burden."

"Have you seen him?" Sam asks. "Has he stood on your property and threatened you?" He explains my rights.

"I don't want such a pleasant afternoon to end on a bad note," I say. "Matt may not even show up. Maybe he called to see if I could be scared into writing him a check. Come on y'all let's get this mess cleaned up and proceed with pleasant thoughts."

Sam places an arm around his wife's waist. "I'm sorry there's nothing I can do for you, Quinn, but you call me if he shows up, you understand?"

"All I ever wanted to do was retire, have a home, grow flowers, do a little reading and make a few friends." I shake my head. "It's not going to be so simple from here on out, is it?"

After the clean-up, I stretch my arms over my head and twist around to loosen my back. As I gather my things, I say, "I'd like to have you both over for supper one evening."

"We'd be delighted. I'm glad you came." Grier responds, "You stay safe, you hear?" She taps my shoulder scanning the cleaned kitchen. "Did today remind you of when we were kids, visiting between our homes?"

I shake my head. "No, I don't remember us making noise or all the busyness. Now we're on the other side of the sound and motion, I guess."

"Granny's cake was wonderful," she says. "I'm dredging up memories just tasting it. I didn't know you had her recipe."

"I wrote Mama for the recipe right after I got married. *Humph*. Like a sweet and sour memory for me now when I look back."

"What do you mean?"

"Well, he always showed me off back then. I enjoyed cooking. When we were out with friends or had company he was always being sweet, but I knew as soon as he downed his second drink, I was in for a long night afterwards." I shudder.

"The cake was wonderful. Maybe this time it will bring you a special magic. Make me a copy of the recipe please, ma'am." Grier gives me a hug.

I slice off half of the remaining cake and hand it to her. "Enjoy this. I'll bring the recipe tomorrow." I rewrap my cake, snap the lid tight on the whipped cream and tuck everything into my basket.

My ears ring with silence as I drive home. I freeze the remaining cake and wonder what life with children would have been like.

My Carolina room calls me to the window. My reflection stares back. The cheek where Jason kissed me feels warm. As the sky begins to darken, I brew a cup of tea and carry a cup into the bedroom for an evening with my books. They scatter on the floor when the phone rings. I pick up the receiver and make a mental note to get a caller ID machine. I cringe. "Hello."

"Have I disturbed you? It's Danny. I wanted to catch you before it gets too late."

"No, I was just settling down with a book. What's up?" I'm pleased he called.

"We're having a church covered-dish supper in my neighborhood Thursday evening. Will you be my guest?" His big green eyes and good company beckon me.

"Sure, let me get my calendar. For someone who's retired I'm getting very busy."

On Thursday evening, Danny picks me up. I made a freezer of ice cream and we balance it on the floor between my feet. His two loaves of warm garlic bread rest on the seat between us.

"I like this. When they started the church suppers, I thought it'd be a drudge. You make it nice." He squeezes my hand. My fingers, cold from the ice cream canister, warm in his clutch.

We're the last couple to arrive. Dave Paterson's paunch and bald head are ever-present at church covered-dish meals. His wife, Lavonia, is a gaunt woman who speaks with a Long Island accent. An obituary about Dave's brother rests in my basket of accidental deaths. The couple is understandably quiet. I reach out to hug him. "Dave, I'm sorry about your family's loss." I hope my words don't spoil his appetite.

"Thank you. The people in the church are so nice with cards and," he pats his stomach, "casseroles." He grins.

We gather at the table and after a blessing sit down to eat. Dave and Lavonia sit opposite us.

He continues, "John's death was a shock. His wife died a little over a year and a half ago. When we saw the patrol car pull into the drive, we thought something happened to one of our kids. I guess we all fear getting that knock at the door."

The other two couple's heads bob like a car's backseat window dogs.

"John was my big brother." He smiles remembering, "He loved going out in his boat. He's usually so careful, you know, watching the weather and wearing a life jacket. I've been out with him, fishing in the very same spot."

He stops for a moment to butter a piece of bread. "I don't understand how he went overboard. He must have hit his head when he fell. Now, I'm dealing with all the paperwork of his estate. I'm executor."

Another man at the table speaks up. "I know about what you're going through. I had to handle my parents' estate last year. We drove to Missouri several times. You can't do everything by phone and mail." He jabs the air with his fork. "I got to one point when I sat on the porch and sobbed. Every time I picked up a familiar object, memories flooded back." He offers, "Dave, can I help you do anything?"

"No, no. We're boxing up and taking things to Goodwill. The strangest thing was they sold the house or something. He didn't say a word to me about it. When he and his wife were living, they bought some annuity-like thing. They swapped their house for lifetime income. It's called a reverse mortgage. They live in their home and receive monthly checks from a company buying their house. When John and his wife die, the mortgage company gets the house. Unfortunately, neither my brother nor his wife lived long enough to enjoy their lifetime income.

"This company notified us we had sixty days to clear out. It was a shock. There's a small settlement check but nothing like what the house is worth. I guess as retirees need more income, reverse mortgages will become more popular."

Dave reaches in his pocket for his handkerchief, wipes his nose and bolsters himself. "Hey, this is really good lasagna, may I have seconds?"

Danny's leg bumps mine and his eyebrows go up. I feel a bit of déjà vu. After the hot tomato pasta main course, my peach ice cream hits the spot. I scoop generous portions into waiting bowls. When Danny drives me home later in the evening, he carries the empty ice cream freezer into the house. He sets it into the sink and turns me around into his arms.

"Quinn Winslow, I've cared about you ever since grade school. I know you feel the same about me." He reaches for my hands. "Being with you again these past few months is like you never left. I want us to be more." He pulls a ring box from his pocket. "Honor me by becoming my wife. I want us to enjoy the rest of our lives together."

I draw back, dumbfounded. I grab his hand as he tries to open the box. "Shush. Don't say another word. I'm not ready, Danny." I hold my arms out, imitating one of those twirly lawn sprinklers. "I need time to get comfortable with this life I've only begun."

"Look, I know you had a bad marriage. I want to make things up to you. I…"

"Danny." How can I explain? "Remember the television program in the fifties, 'I Led Three Lives'? That's how I feel."

He gives me a confused scowl.

"First, I had a wonderful childhood. I'll always cherish those family memories. You were a part of those growing up years and a dear friend. Second, my horrible marriage with Matt destroyed all the happiness in my life, as well as any confidence. You can't imagine the fear of nightly abuse."

"No, I can't, but…" he tries again. He reaches to hold me but I push him away. "You know, there were times when I wanted to kill myself. I actually went to the dresser drawer and felt for his gun in the darkness -- more than once, while Matt slept off another drunk. I thought it was my fault!

"When I asked for a divorce, my parents were devastated. They were ashamed of me and let me know it! Then Daddy died. All my good memories and hopes sank along with his fishing trawler. You weren't around and I don't expect you to know, but Mama died the next year. I was heart-broken. We never made up before they died."

"But you're fine now." He takes my hand again. "We've had a few months of getting to know one another again. Don't ruin our future by your thoughts of the past. We're the same two people."

"It's not all in the past, Danny. Matt called. He thinks he can scare me into paying him to stay away."

"What?"

"He called and said if I didn't pay him there'd be trouble. I'm no longer afraid of him. Back all those years ago I thought I was to blame, making him so brutal." I point to my third finger. "I scrubbed floors and maintained a senior co-op in Raleigh for over thirty years. You have no idea what it's like to try to rebuild your life, always wondering if you're doing the right thing, startled at every loud sound."

I pull him over to the kitchen bar and we sit down. "As I renovated this house, Danny, I restored order in my life. I was certain about every decision I made. At this point, I don't know where I want to go next. I don't know if I want to be married."

He stands, still holding my hands. He shakes his head.

"I'm almost sixty years old," I say. "Now, I live in the town where I grew up, with none of those old fears. I need a while to savor what I have. I'm in control now. You'll always be a friend."

He flinches at the "friend" word, but tight lips a nod as he says his goodbye, "Fair enough, but I'm going to keep hoping and I may ask again." He kisses his fingers and gently touches my cheek. "I'm glad you came with me tonight. Thanks for explaining your reasons. The rejection doesn't sting as much. Guess I'll be going. Good night."

I watch him drive away from my driveway before shutting off the porch light and closing the door. From the kitchen, I see his truck's tail lights disappear when he turns the corner at the end of the block.

SIX

Attending my first Investment Club meeting the next week, I meet Daphne George at her door. "So you're Grier's cousin. I heard you were coming." Daphne scrutinizes my clothes. "Your necklace is nice. Is that real turquoise?" Her lips pucker into a moue. "Turquoise is supposed to be in this year."

"Thank you. The necklace is a family heirloom. As you guessed, I'm Quinn Winslow." I hold out my hand but she ignores it.

The obese peach-haired woman, wearing too much makeup, fans her face. "I don't like anything suggesting the Southwest. It's too hot for me." She doesn't introduce herself or welcome me into her home.

I try to be the good person my Mama taught me to be. "You must be Daphne. What a lovely home. Grier had an errand to run this morning, but she'll be here." I glance into the living room. Eleanor and Kat are bending over the buffet. I just met Daphne and I'm already looking for an escape route.

Daphne leads me across the front landing, pointing out pieces of art and expensive furniture using her floral cane, painted like a Monet garden.

Grier's words come back to me, "Daphne George could make an elephant feel small. Pay her no mind!" My cousin gave me the scoop on her during our morning walk. "In high school Daphne was a cheerleader. She married the college quarterback, collected her college diploma and snuggled herself into high society ranks, like a mama hen takes to her nest. Her perky chubbiness, cute for jumping and cartwheels grew to battleship proportions after her marriage, which unfortunately, has caused her knees to go. A son is studying law to join his father's practice and the daughter is still in college. I feel sorry for Daphne, but she can be so material-girlish."

Daphne swirls through the house in aquamarine slacks and embroidered silk caftan as she shows me her realm. I pay attention to her home tour, but wonder how many silk worms struggled to make all the cloth. She sweeps her arm, "This is my favorite room. Isn't the view remarkable?"

From the third story loft, the 360 degree unobstructed cupola scans both the ocean and sound sides of the island, as well as the natural forest of cedars and live oaks shaped by centuries of ocean winds.

I appreciate the beauty of the coastline. "It is a one of a kind panorama. How lucky for you."

She pants after our climb up the steps. "Luck had nothing to do with it. When I saw this house and the view, I told my husband I wanted it. We bought it from the builder who lived here."

When we return to the first floor, I note the furnishings hint at aloof beachiness. No family pictures stick to the refrigerator with silly magnets nor do any shoes pile at the back door. I can't picture myself stretched out on the white couch or walking barefoot across the blue tiled kitchen floor. She dismisses me when the doorbell rings again.

"Quinn, I'm so glad you decided to join us." Eleanor taps her spoon against her coffee cup. "May I have your attention please?"

Grier sneaks in as the other women turn from the finger food buffet to find chairs in the formal living room. Conversations diminish. Notebooks and pencils appear from bags and purses. Heads dip to review notes before starting the business meeting.

Eleanor, a natural at organizing papers and people, opens the meeting. "Grier, I believe you have a guest." She yields the floor.

Grier stands to introduce me. Having prior information, I recognize names and match them with faces. I wave at Kat and Tricia Lewis, my realtor. The clothes vary from beach casual to haut couture. I count a half dozen pearl necklaces ranging from a ribbon tied string on a pretty young woman wearing a matching cardigan set to the triple stack on Eleanor's neck.

As part of the new business portion of the meeting, Daphne quips, "I'd like my share of Birdie's money, please. Can you print me out a check by the end of the week?"

As Eleanor makes a note, the rest of the members express shock at her request.

"What? It's my share. Why shouldn't I get it now?" Daphne glares back.

When no one responds, she shrugs her shoulders and repositions her caftan over her legs, folding her dough-like hands in her lap. As the meeting continues, she chomps on Danish wedding cookies, which sprinkle a trail of confection sugar down her front. Her cane props against an end table between the linen covered couch and the pale wall. I painted many industrial-white walls when I worked in Raleigh. I'm glad I now live within brightly painted rooms.

As the meeting proceeds, various members give the names and backgrounds of selected companies. Each member discusses her choice of stock purchase or recommendation for a sale. They defend stock positions like arguing barristers.

Observing the others, I realize my consignment rack pick-over clothes feel dumpy, except for Grace's necklace. Grier's offer for a clothes shopping trip sounds better today. Following the business session, we adjourn to a restaurant on the western end of the barrier island. Grier tags a ride with me.

"I left my car at the shop and got a ride here on the shuttle. Hope you don't mind chauffeuring me around."

"My pleasure." I'm delighted to drive her, avoiding another whirl on the road in Grier's Volvo.

When we arrive at the restaurant, Tricia and Grier sit on either side of me. Eleanor sits across the table with another woman.

I ask Tricia, "How did you get into the real estate business?"

"I started selling properties at a time-share office twenty years ago. Look at me now with my face on highway billboards!" She fingers a clutch of gold necklaces. "I've invested in a few pieces of property, but I reward myself with jewelry. See."

She flutters her fingers letting her rings sparkle in the light. Her flaming coiffure, exaggerated by weekly beauty parlor trips, explodes around her face. "But, nobody wants to hear my history. How are you doing? Is the house finished?"

When she sold me the house last fall, she told me about the Help & Hands Shelter. Her broken nose betrays a past similar to mine. She fled from her husband and trailer park life, taking her three boys still in their pajamas, out into a snowy Christmas night.

"It's finished. Come for a visit the next time you're in the neighborhood. I haven't done much entertaining. Grier and Danny Bridges are my only visitors so far." I stop to admire the restaurant, a former Coast Guard Station. "This is a wonderful setting."

Tricia informs me, "The owners purchased the obsolete facility and found Coast Guard memorabilia for the decorations. They stole the chef from some place in the northeast. It's one of my favorite places to bring clients."

We read over the luncheon menu and make our choices.

"I'll have the baked grouper with asparagus and a light lemon sauce. No butter, please. I'm trying to stick with my diet."

Grier smiles at me and orders a chef salad topped with grilled shrimp. I eat everything on my plate, noting both Tricia and Grier don't finish theirs. They push food around with their forks and leave part of their meal untouched.

Begin Again, Quinn

The other member at the table, Alice McNeill, reaches for the last hushpuppy. She sits quietly, until she says, "No sense in this going to waste." She munches the crusty cornbread. "Tricia, can I interrupt you a minute?" She swallows. "I want to sell my house. Can you to list it and show me what's available. I'd like something smaller."

"I had no idea you wanted to sell. Sure, I'll call you later and schedule a time."

To me she says, "Alice was the last to join our group until you came. We've taught her everything she knows about money. Her husband died, what -- three years ago?"

"It's more like twenty-eight months, but who's counting?" Alice volleys back. "I didn't know how to write a check or make money decisions."

I'm surprised at her remark.

Alice pats the tablecloth with her hand. "It's not like you think. Ken was good to me but he ran everything. He chose our house. I've never liked it. He even had the gall to have it decorated without consulting me."

Alice waits for me to acknowledge, then continues. "When he died, I didn't know where our money was, what banks he had it in or anything. He always gave me cash if I needed to buy anything. I was furious with him leaving me so helpless. Without this group, I don't know what I'd have done."

Tricia applauds, "And we're proud of you."

Grier asks, "Do you want another house or are you thinking a townhouse? I hear cluster homes are getting popular here."

"What's a cluster home?" Alice asks. Her eyebrows turn inward as little vertical frown lines appear above her nose.

Tricia answers, "It's like a duplex, but they are connected in a pod sharing common yards. It's a new idea among developers." Eleanor adds her reasons for liking the town house versus a condominium. I explain why I wanted a house of my own. Our comments flow freely, based on our own experiences.

While we talk, Alice touches her face and bouffant hair with pale slender fingers. The pink linen pantsuit matches her nails. She turns to me, "Quinn, getting back to the benefits of this club -- I didn't know anything about investments before I joined. My late husband was in insurance. The money was where I couldn't get to it. When he died, I received a lump sum. I didn't know if I could make it on my own. Since being in the club, I'm a lot more comfortable with making money decisions. You know, because Ken died in an accident, I got double pay-off on his life insurance."

Bingo, another accidental death, but I block it from my mind. I'm somewhat appalled by the conversation, but Tricia and I, both being victims of another sort of husband abuse, understand her need to talk. Later, Grier and I excuse ourselves as the group begins to break up.

Walking out to the car, I say, "I learned a lot and it was only the first meeting. I think I'll join. Also, you said you'd take me shopping. When can we go?"

She pulls out her pocket calendar and we decide to leave early Saturday morning.

I'm washing my supper dishes that evening, when a faded blue sedan pulls into my driveway. Through the windshield, I see the drooping headliner and my former husband. The salad I ate for supper rolls as tight as a tinfoil ball in my stomach. Grabbing the remote phone off the wall, I press in 911 but delay the call dial. I face him at my front door, the phone behind my back.

"Matt, you have no business here."

"Hello to you too, Quinn. Now don't get all huffy with me. I came by to visit a bit. I mentioned a little business we might take care of last week. I hear you got a bundle when your aunt died. She's the one, lived in New Bern, right?" He shrunk since I last saw him, with a new pouch of stomach hanging over a tooled western belt. The black leather vest over a snap front plaid shirt and jeans look like something he'd wear to a rodeo, but I know he can't stand the smell of horses.

He leans with an arm against my door sill and props one booted foot across the other. The odor of generously applied aftershave burns my nose. I actually feel disgust, not fear, as I watch him.

"Nice house you got here, pleasant neighborhood. It would be a shame if…"

"You don't frighten me anymore, Matthew." I stare directly into his eyes. "Turn around and get back in your car."

He tries to pull the screen door open, but the hook holds it shut.

"I took out a restraining order on you thirty years ago." I hold up the phone. "I already dialed 911. All I have to do is move my thumb."

He glares, his jaw working back and forth.

"Go away." My heart beats loudly.

"The court order expired years ago." He smirks. "Aren't we mighty sure of ourselves now? You got a big bad dog in there to chew me up in little pieces, too?" He belches stale beer in my face. "Okay, Sugar Girl." He uses the name he called me in high school when he thought I was so sweet. "I don't want to see you anymore either, but now I got a reason. How about a little check? You won't even miss it."

"There will be no check." I release my thumb.

He holds up his hands, palms out. "I'm leaving you, but," he aims his finger at me as if he's pointing a gun at my head, "I'll get you later." He pretends to fire off a round.

We both can hear the ping of three dialed numbers. I stare back as he stumbles down my front steps.

"Don't be surprised if I sneak up on you one day when you're working in that pretty back yard of yours." He takes a couple of long-legged strides.

I hear the phone ringing.

"This is the 911 emergency number, what is the nature of your call?"

He hollers back at me, "I like what you've done in your back room. I saw the picture of your parents on the side table. Nice, real nice." The car door screeches as he pulls it open. "Wouldn't want anything to happen to your pretty new house, would you?" He drives away as the responder asks me again why I called.

I explain the circumstances and two officers arrive within minutes. "He threatened me on my porch, tried to come into my home, uninvited. He said he would do something to my house if I didn't pay him."

The officers take the information and leave. I practice my deep breathing, as I say a prayer. If nothing else, my ex-husband provokes frequent prayer on my part. Afterwards, I fix myself a cup of tea and hook up the new caller ID phones in the bedroom and kitchen. I program both phones to call 911 with a one finger touch.

###

Grier arrives promptly Saturday smelling of lilacs and sandalwood.

Buckling in, I say, "*Mmm*, someone got a new perfume."

"Yeah," she says. "You like it?" She pulls out a James Taylor CD and slides it into her player. "I have today all planned, so sit back and enjoy. Rosemary St. Clair's clothes are not your usual 'little old lady' knit sportswear and Sunday dresses. She specializes in comfortable clothes. I've been going there for years."

"Why do I have a feeling this is going to break my pickle jar wardrobe budget?" I giggle. "However, today, I'm prepared to put a dent in the checking account."

"A pickle jar? I remember." She laughs and draws the conversation back to clothes.

"Rosemary designs a whole line of vests, shirts and funky things. I'm a walking ad for her," Grier pinches her pants, pulling the fabric away from her leg. Her cropped pants match her lime tweed top. "This is going to be a shopping extravaganza."

During our forty-minute drive to New Bern, I break the news about Matt's re-appearance.

She's surprised he came by so quickly. "You're all grown up now and he can't hurt you. You know that, don't you?"

"Easy to say that, but the delivery and follow through is questionable. I'm taking it one sighting at a time."

"Good for you."

I feign assurances and dig deep inside to drag up my lagging confidence as my heart drums 'call to arms.'

She reaches over and gives my hand a tug. "I'm here if you need me, Shug."

We find a parking spot not far from the pre-Revolutionary War Tryon Palace and forget Matt. The New Bern Historical Society rebuilt the former governor's home using the original plans from the 1700's. Beautiful gardens and Colonial era homes encircle the neighborhood. Authentically dressed docents guide tourists through the buildings, much like Williamsburg, Virginia. Tongue tempting whiffs from a nearby cafe mingle with the heat of the morning. We climb porch steps where several mannequins display beautiful outfits and jewelry.

A smiling red-haired woman throws out her arms to welcome us when we ring the doorbell. "No one else is here yet. You have my undivided attention." Her store occupies the front rooms of her living quarters, half of a red clapboard turn-of-the-century two-story duplex. "How can I help?"

After receiving Grier's challenge to "dress" me, Rosemary eyes me critically. She pulls several pieces of clothing from racks and drawers, gathering garments while maintaining a constant monologue. "Grier, it's good to see you. How are those grandbabies?"

The markdown rack draws my attention. Rosemary follows, "You'll love this fabric. You wash it on gentle cycle and add vinegar. That keeps the colors bright. Here, midnight blue is your color." She carries an armful of clothes back to the dressing room.

"Now we're going for size first, then we'll pick the colors. Here's a skirt, slacks, two tops and this vest or the jacket matches it. The black sheath, you can do so much with it."

She notes Grier's outfit. "Go stand on the porch and be one of my models!" She laughs and turns back to me. "When the weather cools or warms you add or take off layers." She gently pushes me into the dressing room.

Thank God, Mama taught me to wear good underwear when I go clothes shopping. Before stepping behind the curtain, Rosemary picks up a set of shoulder pads and snaps a pincushion to her wrist.

She talks with pins held between her lips. "This needs shoulder pads, dear."

She returns with an assortment of colors and styles. After trying on each selection, I march out for approval. "Grier, what do you think?"

"*Ooowah*, I like that on you." or "No, the jacket hits you in the widest part of your butt. Get the longer one." Grier validates my favorites.

Begin Again, Quinn

Two hours later, I feel like I've tried on everything in the store. A few more customers have come and left. I'm still trying on clothes. I'm confident with the purple, blue and green stacks of clothes on the counter.

"This makes so much sense. Even I can mix and match." I wear a new tunic and slack set. "I think this is a funny mirror. I look pounds thinner. I'm going to wear this. Can you take the tags off?"

"Honey, you are thinner since we started walking," Grier tells me.

With Grier watching, I pay for it all. I don't even blink when I write the three-figure check. We carry the decorated clothes bags outside to the car.

"Didn't I tell you she's fantastic? Those clothes will never wear out and they travel so well. When I can talk you into going away, we may take a cruise or something with the other girls. Wouldn't that be fun?"

"Whoa, one step at a time. I'm not ready for a cruise yet."

"No? Well anyway, it's something to think about. I'd like to go to Bermuda. Doesn't it sound inviting? I've always wanted to do that."

My stomach growls.

"Is that you?"

"I didn't eat much breakfast, sorry."

"We're ready for lunch, then." We lock our purchases in the trunk and walk over to Chadwick's Cafe.

Other patrons at the restaurant include a group of Red Hat Ladies. For one somber moment, I wonder if I'll be clipping any of them from our weekly paper in the near future. It's easier to reconcile obituary names without faces.

I pay our bill. "I insist, don't quibble. You drove. It's my treat." We wander up the street. "I haven't shopped in New Bern in years."

Grier updates me. "The town went downhill after the mall was built twenty years ago. The Downtown Association worked to draw locals and tourists in for shopping and a bit of history." She points along the street. "There used to be department stores and dime stores, but today the main streets offer antique stores, boutique shopping and galleries. We walk pass a black wrought iron fence enclosing a church yard. Children climb on a colorful slide and monkey bars. "Children visit the totlot, that's a new word in the dictionary according to my son, while parents tag-team from one store to another. Come on, I want to show you another favorite place." Grier grabs my arm and leads me across the street where a fountain gurgles in an alley. She opens the door to a remodeled storefront.

Carolina Creations offers local artists' handiwork across the street from the 18th century Episcopal Church. "Look at these paintings. They have the most unique pottery and jewelry."

"What a clever display," I say. Raku pots and platters line one wall among shelving and shadow boxes of art. Across the room paintings by local artists hang. Glassware, pottery, paintings, decorated leather and books are arranged on attractive Lucite and wooden shelving. "These are beautiful and useful, too." A pewter spoon rest catches my eye. I also purchase a package of note cards and a vase.

The main street offers more gift and clothing stores. We pass benches and huge carved wooden bears in a park, conveniently located for children and tired shoppers. Grier leads me back toward the car. "Here's one of my favorite stops, Mitchell Hardware. They have everything, even the missing sprinkler head for my weed sprayer."

The church bell strikes four as we return to the car. "Whew, I definitely shopped until I dropped!"

I relax in the leather seats of the Volvo sedan. We seldom ride in it since Grier usually drives the station wagon. She doesn't glimpse over her shoulder as she pulls into the traffic. I sink down in my seat, cringing as a car honks at us.

Begin Again, Quinn

Grier crosses the Trent River Bridge, slipping under red bridge-opening warning lights. She zooms toward Morehead City. Not wanting to pay attention to the road while Grier makes havoc of the highway, I mentally begin to weed my closet.

Mama used to make all my clothes when I was in school. I wore them with pride. With my outside looking good, now I'll work on my mind and comfort levels.

SEVEN

In the past two weeks, I've met Charles' financial advisor protégée, Investment Club members and distanced myself from Danny. With no word or appearance from Matt, I'm beginning to relax at home in the evenings when I'm alone. Side trips with Grier and new friends replace my routine of working on the house.

Twice a week, I volunteer at the Help & Hands Domestic Violence Center. The counseling sessions heal old wounds I still feel. Discarded children and spouses end up at the Center. The one-story building, a former school, deserted after integration and updated by local and state monies, offers shelter for the abused. The cement block exterior has a new coat of paint. The acrid smell of roofing repairs greets me when I park in the lot beside the front door. Today I hear Latino music coming from the radio balanced on the scaffolding. The workmen banter as they spread the hot sticky tar-like goop.

The fluttering flag causes the halyard to clatter against the pole. Gardeners, a group of various sized and aged women, are planting annuals along the walkway to the office. I smolder at the sight of fresh bruises or cuts. One woman with an arm cast stands alone watching the others.

Each room inside has a different activity or class to help the women and children piece back their lives. Curtis Tulley, an African American security guard, opens the door for me.

"Good morning Ms. Winslow."

"Good morning, Curtis. Did you have a good weekend?" I ask.

He scratches his cropped hair and tells me about his grandchildren's visit. He shakes his round face. "Glad to see they come and glad to see they go," he chuckles. He worked with the sheriff's department before he retired to work for the Center. His daughter was a client a few years ago. She now runs her own florist business in town.

Begin Again, Quinn

I wave back at him as I head for my room. A bread baking aroma greets me in the central hall. Alberta Taylor runs the kitchen from her wheel chair. The bakery and catering business pays a portion of the center's operating expenses. Fresh breads, soups, sauces and meals-to-go are available for customers who drop by on their way home from work.

The electrical shop rewires fans, lamps and kitchen appliances for use or resale. The smell of soldering stings my nose as I pass. Derelict small appliances await their resurrection on waist-high tables. We have our own retail store. Our clients learn shop skills and how to deal with customers. College students, rental property owners and newlyweds find bargains furnishing their homes with the Center's recyclables.

There's also a computer, business and medical office classroom. A carpentry work area abuts the gymnasium where I work. I stop as Marguerite Peterson, the facility director, leaves the playschool area.

"Oh, good, I'm glad I caught you. We need to talk about a new person in your furniture repair class." She smokes secretly, but her cough and deep voice betray the habit. Marguerite's skin is dark, like semi-sweet chocolate. She's a tough, no nonsense administrator who bargains effectively for funds and intuitively knows whether to pull out her kid gloves or crow bar.

Over her silk blouse and tailored slacks, she wraps a smock with her name embroidered on the pocket. We all wear smocks in this building. It helps to identify with members of our group.

Marguerite says, "Tomorrow Mayberry is new. That's her real name. When the mother left the child at her grandmother's, she said she'd be back tomorrow. She never came back, but the name stuck. She's supposed to be in school, but got herself suspended again, a problem with her attitude. When her grandmother works, Tomorrow comes here to work, but usually she curls up on a couch and shields herself with a snotty attitude. Her only ambition in life is to bother people."

In the background, happy children in colorful clothes play duck, duck, goose, but as Marguerite talks the joy of the surroundings fade from her face. "A man claiming to be her father showed up and she moved in with him for a while. When she was ten years old, she was picked up for shoplifting. She went back to live with her grandmother, but it didn't work out. Two years ago, they arrested her father, at the school Halloween Carnival for pimping her out of the men's restroom. She was fourteen!"

"Oh, my Lord."

"The system let her fall through the cracks. Anyhow, I wanted to give you a heads up before you get to your classroom." She touches my arm. "I know she can learn if she puts her mind to it. See what you can do with her." Marguerite nods and strides down the hall with something or someone else on her mind.

I have a dozen ladies, all ages, colors and backgrounds in my classroom. Some stay in my class and never move on to other classes. Some work on their own projects. I spy the girl immediately. She slumps on a couch alone, thin arms crossed defiantly across her chest. Her chin shoves out a permanent don't-mess-with-me pose.

"Morning everyone." I reach for my denim smock, place my purse in one of the multiple cubbyhole shelves we use for personal items and turn to evaluate the furniture rejects. The center gets broken furniture from the Salvation Army and Habitat for Humanity. When pieces are broken but repairable, they haul it to us instead of taking it to the dump.

"Let's do some woodworking. Can I get a little help?"

We pull a love seat, matching side chair and a pair of end tables to the center of the floor. I explain why they're worth repairing, pointing out the good wood, dove-tail joints and basic lines. "You need to know how to identify the good stuff from the particle board and poor construction pieces," I say.

Sandpaper and cleaners selected, my regulars begin their work. Pulling a three-legged stool from the stack, I approach Tomorrow.

Begin Again, Quinn

"Hello, I'm Quinn. You and this stool need to get acquainted." I give her sandpaper. "I've found you can work on your thoughts and feelings while sanding. Try it," I encourage.

She sulks, grimacing as she turns the stool and gritty paper in her hands. Her bitten down nails are painted lavender to match her tank top and baggy shorts. Cigarette burns, or that's what they look like scar several spots on her caramel-colored arms and legs.

"We have smocks to keep your clothes clean by the cubby boxes if you want one," I suggest.

She stares through me, until I walk away.

Within the hour, wiping saw dust off my nose, I notice she is working on the hard linoleum floor. She sits on a folded smock. Her long thin legs straddle the stool. Saw dust covers her legs and arms. A wiry hair halo moves in time with her arms.

"Good work everyone. Let's take a break."

We eat lunch at noon. I meet Tricia Lewis in the breakroom. She has more energy than a passel of puppies. She sits down with diet soda and plastic-wrapped salad. Twice a month, she comes to teach about county agencies, government services, medical and legal aid.

I ask, "How do you do all the things you do? You're so successful, confident. I'm envious."

She gives me a bit of history filling in the blanks. "I raised three sons by myself. If you want to hear horror stories, I'll tell you about the drugs, teen pregnancies and resentments my three boys shared. As for my journey, a grant at the community college paid for childcare and my tuition. I'd reached bottom."

I nod my head. "I've been at that bottom."

"It takes a lot of guts to break away, doesn't it?"

"I don't know if I'd still be alive if I had stayed in my marriage. I ran." The memory still hurts. "I regret getting married or dating him in the first place. When we were young, we didn't have many choices after high school. You went to college if you had the brains and the money, or worked at the shirt factory, or…"

She finishes, "We got married to our high school sweethearts!"

"Matt is pestering me again. He's not hurt me or anything," I confide.

"You'll be fine. You were smart in school. I bet you've learned a lot over the years."

"Piffle," I say. "Smart didn't help when I believed I was a failure. He literally hammered it into me for five long years. I still carry those insecurities dealing with people, especially men. I know how to react, but putting it to practice is another step. I still jump if the door slams."

"Quinn, you're a grown woman. You're accomplished. You have money now. You have respect here at the Center." Tricia puts her fork down and waits.

"My biggest problem is I can't get over this divorce thing. My parents taught me divorce was a sin." I pick up my sandwich. "They made marriage look easy."

"It's not a pretty load. You need to find a place to dump it." Tricia leans as she hikes her leg up under herself on the chair.

"I know my parents are frowning down at me. A marriage is a commitment for life and I ran away from mine. No one got divorced back then. I thought if I prayed harder, or if I were a better wife, the marriage would be better. I thought I could change him."

"That was your first mistake. You can't change them." Tricia snorts. "It wasn't you or the marriage, dear. It was your controlling husband. Admit it. He abused you."

"I started working here because I needed to face my ghosts."

"I learned all over again, the things I should have learned in school," Tricia says. "I'm here volunteering because I never had anything like this." She clears invisible crumbs off the table. "Once I got the money-making part down, I found there were other areas needing improvement. I hired a speech teacher for diction."

"Did you really?" I think that's weird.

"All these Yankees come down here and they didn't understand me so I learned how to talk all over again. It must have worked. Sales increased with out-of-staters. I even hired a personal trainer."

"You look great."

"That's enough about our past. It's behind us. What are you doing now you have the house finished?"

I take a bite out of my Subway special and chew as I word my thoughts.

"I'd have to make a list, but let me ask you a question. I've been thinking about something for the past few weeks. Do you ever get involved in reverse mortgages?" I watch her reaction.

"Nope, not what I do. I've lost a couple of listings to a Raleigh company. There's too much on my plate. Right now, I'm waiting to see if I can list Margaret Byrd's house."

Margaret Byrd, like a flash card, pops up again. "Really, tell me more." I get up for a bottle of water.

"I need a chance to make my pitch to her heirs, can't move too soon. In my business, you have to watch who's getting the sales. When a big one's out there, I know." Every red hair is in place, subtle makeup, even without her jacket, wearing a smock over her clothes, she portrays confidence.

"Do you want a reverse mortgage?" She fiddles with her grilled chicken strips in her salad. "Usually people with limited income and assets go for it. I've gone to a couple of seminars. My partner researched them, but I can get you some information."

"Reverse mortgages were mentioned the other night. Danny Bridges says someone is killing old people and making it look like an accident, like Margaret Byrd. Then a man at our church mentioned how a reverse mortgage company took over his brother's house before grass sprouted on his grave. His brother was a widower who died in a boating accident."

"*Ooowah*, playing detective are you? So you think someone killed Margaret. You need motive. The police didn't find anything suspicious, did they?"

"No. I've been collecting death notices. You'd be surprised at the number of accidental deaths among people over fifty-five."

"I always thought heart disease or cancer would get most of us."

"And another thing, how about the club's right-of-survivorship clause?" I point out. "Have you ever thought someone would take advantage of it?"

"*Hmm.* I see where you're going here. You already met a club member who spends more money than she has." Tricia winks at me, over her salad. "Gossip says her husband has her on an allowance. He took away all her charge cards. Maybe Daphne did Birdie in to get to our investment pool." Trisha sits back in her seat still avoiding her lunch. "Margaret Byrd invested a lot of money with the club. Getting rid of her leaves more money for us, if you get my drift." She pokes her fork at chunks of tomato and cucumbers. Daphne asked Eleanor for her share last week."

Tricia takes a long sip on her drink and adds another thought. "Another suspect to think about -- do you know Lee Kelson? He's Kat Knowles' nephew. Last week several of us played bridge at her house, when this nephew, Lee, called up on the phone. I only heard one side of the conversation but he wanted money from her and I'm not talking pocket change. Boy, Kat was upset. He's in some kind of a financial bind."

"What makes him think he can do that?"

"Kat says he's her heir, but she's not ready to turn over any of her retirement savings," Tricia says.

"And well she shouldn't. I just met her and I can't imagine having kin who would -- oh yeah. Matthew would." I sigh.

"Lee Kelson and his parents moved down here not long after Kat and her husband. When both his parents died, he spent all his inheritance then looked around to find his Aunt Katherine. He sidled up to her, started visiting and sweet talking her. Now he's her cat's meow."

"Can't she see what he's doing?"

"Yeah, but who else does she have? She's affectionate and has no children of her own."

"And you think he knows enough about the club finances to finagle funds from the investment pool?"

"I guess he figures with Katherine having a bigger portion, he can get her to sell off some and give it to him." Her red eyebrows climb up into her bangs. "He's developing home sites from big estates." She chomps a piece of lettuce. "He's a slick little weasel."

The Nancy Drew in me starts to paint a confusing picture. I continue to chew on my sandwich and Tricia's words. "So what you're saying is not only Kat's nephew wants cash, but also a member of the club, like Daphne, might have an incentive to encourage Margaret's death?"

Tricia picks at her salad, "Yep and the way the real estate market is picking up, you could add me to your list of suspects. I love getting my hands on a lovely old family home listing. I make big bucks handling the sale or putting it into a real estate investor's hands for development. Bing-bing-bang." She swipes her hands together and her bracelets jangle for emphasis. "I turn a tidy profit," she smiles at her own shrewdness.

Now she fidgets with her crackers. Why don't skinny people just eat and quit playing with their food?

"I'm kidding, of course, about me and killing someone for profit. I think Danny's egging you on. By the way, are you still seeing him?"

I squirm. "I'm not seeing Danny. We're just good friends. Honestly, between you and Grier, you'd think I'm wearing an advertisement like, 'single wealthy older woman seeks companionship.' Okay, I'll stop with the murder mystery if you stop with the matchmaking."

We finish our lunch and return to our respective classes. The afternoon sun heats up the old gym. I turn on a couple of fans. My students usually bring their lunch or heat something in the kitchen. Tomorrow browses the edge of the room brailing the block walls with her fingers.

"Did you get something to eat?" I ask.

"Ms. Emily in the kitchen fixed me something. I wadn't hungry no way." She turns and bumps her back against the wall in a steady rhythm, again with the crossed arms.

I take a glue gun from the rack and show her how to brace her stool legs for gluing. She does it so well, I send her off to re-glue the legs and supports on the other furniture. My day finishes around three.

Karen Dodd

Following Kat Knowles' advice, I signed up for a computer class. Before leaving, I change into one of my new outfits. I want to browse the office supply store without sawdust and stain remover on my clothes. A discount coupon is burning a hole in my pocket. I plan on buying myself a computer.

Curtis stands across the doorway as I try to leave. "Know anyone in an old blue Buick?" he asks.

"What!" Heat rises in my face.

"I thought so. He followed you here this morning and every now and then, he glides by. If he parks I amble his way, but he's gone before I get to the curb." He raises his eyebrow.

"My former husband has become a bother recently. He thinks he can scare me. I guess stalking is his new weapon. Thanks for the heads up."

###

When I arrive home, I struggle with the largest box in my car trunk. Charles walks up quietly and puts his hand on my shoulder. I nearly jump out of my shoes.

"Sorry, I didn't mean to spook you. I came to help. Here, move aside. Let me at it."

"Oh, you don't have to." I don't want him hurting his back again. He stands so close to me, I smell his after-shave. "Look here. It has side grab-holes. I'll take one." I'm surprised he's offering, because he never initiated conversation or assistance before. "I signed up for a computer class at the college. I decided to go ahead and get one." I fish the keys out of my purse and open the front door. "You haven't seen the house. Put it on the kitchen counter."

He places the hard drive down and surveys my home's interior. He stoops to run his hand over the hardwood floors. "You refinished these floors, didn't you? Nice job." He stands, "I don't know about the color of the walls. Is it purple or rose or is it the light?" He scrutinizes the edge on one section. "Oh, it's more than one shade from here to the corner."

"Yep, I did the floors first and painted each section of the wall a different shade of purple. It picks up the light as the sun moves around the house.

He peers up at the skylight. "The tube light makes this entry brighter. I like it."

"I'm surprised you noticed. Look around if you like. I'll get the rest. It's not heavy."

"No, no, since I'm here, I may as well do it. You got any coffee?" The front screen slams as he heads back out to my car.

I can't believe he wants to visit. I hurry to the kitchen, measure out coffee, push the start button and remember the frozen cake. I slice off two pieces of Granny's orange cake and zap it a few seconds in the microwave.

By the time he's back, the carafe is filling. "Where do you want this other?"

I show him the corner desk in the guest bedroom. He returns to the car for the printer.

"Thank you, Charles. I've wanted to tell you again, how much I appreciated you allowing me in your house when mine was such a mess. I'm grateful."

"No problem. Glad to be of service."

"Go on into the back room. I call it my Carolina room." I pour two mugs of coffee and place them on a tray with the cake. "Do you take cream or sugar?"

He doesn't answer. I'm afraid to ask again. The setting sun streaks the sky putting a glow on my garden. A gentle breeze blows through the row of open windows.

"What gave you the notion to knock out the wall and extend this room? Great idea, by the way. You must have experience in this kind of thing." His gruffness dissolves. "My house has the same floor plan. It certainly gives me something to think about."

"I did similar work before I moved here. I used to tear pictures out of magazines for my dream house and kept them in a notebook. Many of those ideas went into this house."

Charles takes a long swallow of the coffee. "Good coffee."

"Thank you." I feel heat rising from my neck up to my face. It's not coming from the coffee mug in my hands. I try unsuccessfully to swallow the color off my face. "When I looked at the house the very first time, I knew this was it." Words gush out of my mouth. "It had so much potential."

He breaks off a piece of cake and pops it into his mouth. "*Umm*, I like the orange flavor. Where did you buy it?"

"I made it." I blush once more, "Thank you, again."

"I've been meaning to ask you about your business with the financial planner. How did it go? What about that investment club?" He sits back in the wicker chair as if he's enjoying the view, the snack and my company.

"Very well. I'm glad you gave me her name. I have a better understanding of the market now and a good advisor. I've been busy reading the books you mentioned." I take a breath to slow down my speech. " Next year I start drawing on the IRA I inherited."

My blouse climbs above my stomach when I sit on the couch. I pull it down, "The Golden Girls' Investment Club is interesting, lots of information and personalities. That's another reason I got a computer." I'm amazed Charles is still sitting with me.

"Wonderful view," he points his chin out to the garden, licking his fingers. It's so undignified for Charles. "You did about all the work, didn't you?"

"Yep, the house and the garden -- I moved the bulbs and planted new ones last fall. Two sisters lived in Raleigh where I used to work. They were retired college professors, from Shaw University. They taught me all about annuals and flower gardens. Some of the bulbs I planted out there came from their original stock."

His eyebrows go up with this new information.

"Grier Dew's son, Sam, did the kitchen and bath plumbing, though. I hired someone to do the siding."

We sit in silence enjoying the coffee and the view. It reminds me of the times Mama and Daddy would sit, say nothing and enjoy the moment. Bells go off in my head. What am I thinking?

Charles leans forward to stare at my oriental rug. "Pretty colors. You picked them up for the walls, didn't you?"

"Yes."

As he munches the final bite of cake, he wipes his hand on the napkin. "What is this I'm eating? Nuts and oranges? What's the icing?" He gets up to study my garden. A trellis blocks the view from his side of the fence. Rose tendrils are making their way up to the high points of the barrier.

"It's my grandmother's recipe. There are dates in it, too. The icing is sugar mixed with fresh orange juice. You have to pour it over the cake before it cools. It crinkles the sugar when the cake is warm."

"*Hmm*, best I ever had. How about I help you set up your computer while I have another piece of cake. Is there more coffee?" He heads for the computer.

I refresh our coffee, still not believing I've held his company for a half hour. I cut and wrap a hunk of cake for him to take home.

I call to him from the kitchen. "I've wrapped a piece of cake for you to take home, Charles." I slice another slab for him and a smaller one for myself.

He clears a space for the monitor carton, reaches for his Swiss Army knife and cuts the tape around the edge of the box. "Get some surge protectors next time you go to the Plaza. Are you getting an internet service?"

"I don't know. What do you use?"

"I use the cable company's, but check around." He slides the screen from the box and eases it from the Styrofoam nest. "You want to avoid having your phone line tied up while you're on the computer."

"I'll remember." I read the instruction card and unwrap the cords.

He tackles the tower plug-ins and printer. We work quietly, matching plugs with color-coded inserts. He sinks down on his hands and knees to run the cable beneath the desk.

"Feed the cords down," he directs me. He tugs one. "Which one is this?"

Dangling each cord, I tell him where they connect. I follow his orders, like a good soldier, before tearing open a package of paper and aligning it in the printer.

"Okay, turn it on." He eats his last piece of cake, watching me roll forward in my chair to reach the switch.

"This is exciting. Without your help, I'd probably still be struggling, getting it out of the box."

The computer screen blinks. The machine rumbles and the printer jumps. I feel like a chipmunk with full cheeks, finding another acorn. I ruin it all by saying, "Can I fix you supper to pay back for all…?"

"No!" He bangs his mug down. "Why is it women want to invite me to dinner? When I moved here, every single woman sniffing for a husband sent brownies and casseroles. I almost quit going to church because of all the old biddies. I felt like I had a target painted on my back. I'm not in the market for a wife! Not interested. When will you people understand?"

He stomps out of the room heading for the front door. I follow. My face drains of color at his reaction. Glancing back, he hesitates. I point to the cake sitting on the counter. His face softens as he snatches up the package.

"Thanks for the coffee and the cake. I do like what you've done to the house." He throws an offhand salute, turns and marches back to his yard, careful not to slam the door when he leaves.

Hmm, a step in the right direction, if you call two steps up and one step back a direction. I go back to turn off the computer and clean up our dishes.

Leaving for Help & Hands this morning, I didn't have time to read the paper. The first thing I see when I unfold the newspaper is this notice in classifieds.

"Executor's Notice: North Carolina

Carteret County in the general Court

of Justice of Superior Division

Estate of: Cassie P. Overton

Having qualified as executor of the Cassie P. Overton estate of Carteret County, North Carolina, this is to notify all persons having claims against the estate of Cassie P. Overton, to present them to the undersigned within three (3) months from the date of the publication of this notice, or the same will be pleaded and bar the recovery. All persons indebted to said estate please make immediate payment.

George Davis, Executor of the Cassie P. Overton Estate

c/o Davis and Stanley Law Offices

PO Box 1052, Beaufort, NC 28516 (252)755-1022"

I remember reading about her death. She ran off the road in Georgia on her way to a Florida home. The warmth from my coffee and Charles' company slips away.

He cuts out the notice from the paper and throws the remains into the trash can. Sliding it between the edges of the plastic sleeve, he remembers the first time he used the boyfriend angle. Single old women are so gullible.

Yes, Miss Cassie was unique. From a distance she appeared younger than seventy-six. He pretended to bump into her at a Singles Club. After apologizing, he bought her a drink and started talking the dating get-acquainted silliness. She batted her fake eyelashes, as if she were forty years younger.

Cassie told him she went to a timeshare in Boca Raton, Florida every February. She said it was something her children could use after she was gone. He played the suitor while being her guest in Florida for a couple of weeks. While sitting by the pool, she read Cosmopolitan magazines as eager as any debutante.

She kept her sagging skin neatly tucked into splashy flowered slacks and wore tank tops under see-through blouses to hide the age spots on her arms. Oh, how Cassie loved to dance. They danced and played bridge until he thought he would drown her in the swimming pool in front of everyone.

"Three husbands," Cassie said, "I survived three husbands and too many boyfriends to count." She laughed her nicotine flavored laugh and toasted their relationship. Wide black liner outlined her eyes. She smeared a wedge of lipstick around her mouth. More than once, it ended up on her caffeine-stained teeth.

She should have taken a plane down the last time. Long distance driving was not her forte'. He told her he couldn't come with her, carefully plotting her murder. When he showed up the day she was leaving, she laughed her deep throated laugh. The side trip through the Georgia marshland was his idea. People say you shouldn't try to drive a fifteen-hour trip non-stop. Accidents happen.

Begin Again, Quinn

EIGHT

As another newspaper death notice drops into my pine needle woven basket, I wonder if they do relate to Margaret Byrd's death. I take my phone, a cup of coffee and what remains of my paper, out to the front porch. The phone rings. Checking the caller ID, I see Kat's name. "Hello."

"Quinn? It's Kat Knowles. I'm having a little party after golf on Wednesday. I want you to come. Several of us are playing that morning, but we should be at the clubhouse about 11:30. I hope you can make it."

"Sounds like fun." I go inside to check my calendar. "That's the thirteenth at the Bogue Banks Country Club."

"Yes, the one at Pine Knoll Shores."

"There are several golf courses in the area. I want to get the right one."

"Yes, you got it. Oh and don't bring anything. The others know it's my birthday but I don't want any fuss." She sighs. "I'm so glad we met at the library. I feel like I have a new sister with you, now. The Investment Club girls are the only family I have left, except for my nephew. Oh and the meal is my treat. I insist." She's firm so I don't argue.

"Fair enough. I'll be there with bells on!" I hang up and go back to the paper on the front porch.

Speaking of bells, Charles is coming up the walkway with silverware tinkling against glass baubles. A wind chime dangles from his outstretched hand.

"Morning, neighbor." I prop my cheek up on my palm and grin. "What you got there?"

He props a foot on my step and holds out his offering. "I ran out of coffee this morning. The clerk at the Quick Stop had these hanging above her head with a fan blowing them. I got one for you." He reminds me of a cat dropping a dead cricket on the doormat. "I hope you like it."

"It's lovely. Come sit a minute. I'll get you some coffee." Before he has a chance to back away, I step inside, pour him a big mug of coffee and grab a nail and hammer from my kitchen dump-all drawer. I set a mug of black coffee on the table. "Let me just climb up on this chair so we can enjoy it." With one foot on the chair, I hoist myself up, but my bedroom slipper slides off, tripping me. "*Oof*!"

In slow motion, I see my backside preceding me as hands and arms go flying with hammer waving. I try not to knock Charles in the head. The wind chimes land on my chest as he catches me in a tight grip. When I find my breath, I'm relieved to feel the hammer dangling from one hand, with the nail still clutched in the other hand, which remains around his neck. I feel like I fell against a tree with outstretched arms.

"Are you all right?" He seems mildly amused. "You don't have to do everything, you know. I know you're capable of knocking a nail into the overhang, but how about letting me give it a try?"

His morning tooth paste and shaving cream swarm my olfactory sensor. If I were a swooning woman, this would be the time. Surprised, I spring away from him.

Charles ignores me. "Give me the hammer. I can do this, no charge." He gives me the chimes and steps up on the chair. "Right about here, okay?" He taps the nail in and exchanges his hammer for my new chimes. "This about right?"

I take the hammer and watch as the sunlight cuts through the glass creating jumping colored specks across the porch. On cue, a breeze stirs the tinkling. "I love them, Charles. Who would have thought of taking old spoons and forks? I love them -- absolutely love them." I pull another chair to my table. "Sit down, enjoy your coffee." This is our first chat since he ran off the previous week.

"I'm not much on socializing. Guess it's a Southern thing." He takes a long sip as if he's trying to decide on sharing his thoughts. "The North side of Boston, where I came from, you don't get to know your neighbors, much less want to," he huffs.

"Well, down here, you get to know your neighbors." I crook my head out to the street, "We knew everyone on our street when I was growing up."

"I've stayed to myself since I moved down. My practice kept me busy, still go to Rotary. I'm afraid I've not been a good neighbor since you came."

"You were a big help when my phone went out. I don't know what I'd have done." I want to pat his hand, but resist the urge. "The past few months, I've been too busy redoing the house to socialize." I shrug my shoulders. "Now we'll get to know each other better."

He chews on his bottom lip and then rubs his chin with his hand. "When my wife died, I wasn't interested in meeting other women. We had a good marriage, you see. Her death left a deep space in here." He thumps his chest and pauses. "When I moved down here and joined the church, I couldn't believe there was such an interest in one single man. Even in my business, women came for their first appointment to look me over. I was single and women showed no respect for my privacy… "

"That's too bad. I'm sorry about their poor manners. My past marriage," I take a deep breath, "was not a good experience. I'm glad for your memories, Charles. I'm sorry for your loss." Revealing a bit more of my secrets, I say, "I was so afraid of men after my divorce I avoided them, too, for a different reason of course."

"No," he politely says. "Don't try to smooth over my faults. My stomping out the other day was me being rude. It was a reflex. I apologize. Please accept it with my peace offering. It's a trinket, no trouble to get it for you." He chuckles. "I finished off your cake that evening,"

The pleasant smell of his aftershave creeps across the table. He didn't work in the garden this morning. Seeing him dressed in nice clothes is a pleasant surprise from his gardening duds. I study his clean-shaven face. His square chin has a small cleft. His long straight nose has a little bump on the ridge. His gray eyes look like they could pierce metal, but his bushy eyebrows soften his features.

"How are the crops?" In the past, getting a conversation from him was like pulling teeth. "What all are you growing -- got any tomatoes yet?"

"Little early for tomatoes. The blossoms are out. I got early beans, spring lettuce and cucumbers, plenty to share. Want some?" He moves as if he's going to run over and pull some right now, so I grab his hand. It's a warm comfortable hand.

"Not now, Charles. You can bring me some later if you want. Don't you get dirty on my account."

"I even made a batch of pickles. I wanted to try out a recipe. The recipe called them refrigerator pickles. I think you call them bread and butter pickles down here. I used onions, peppers and cucumbers."

He gently taps my hand with his finger as he speaks. Now I know what a computer mouse feels like.

"Can I heat up your coffee?"

"This is fine. Don't get up." He takes a long swallow. I realize he's left handed. He still wears his wedding band.

"Do you have family in Boston?"

"A brother, he's married with grown children. I haven't heard from him in a while. We stopped sending Christmas cards years ago. I don't remember what got up his dander. I said something about his boys when they were teenagers." Charles makes a sour face. "My wife and I never had children. Guess I overreacted to something and spoke my mind." Creases mar his forehead and he pushes his lips up in thought. His eyebrows almost touch. "I've thought a time or two, to telephone him."

"Call him. I admit I should have called Grier, my cousin and my Aunt Grace and come to see them, but I didn't.

Pride got in my way. You shouldn't let family slip away. They're too important. By the way, you're certainly dressed up today."

"Rotary. It's a bunch of old men getting together to chew the fat, so to speak. I met Hank Morrison the first time I went to Rotary after I moved down here and we have lunch now every week. Dr. Hank Morrison, have you heard of him?"

"Don't believe so. I haven't had time to see a doctor. That reminds me I need to look for a health insurance company."

"Well, he's hired a new associate. We go to lunch as often as he can get away from the office. We kid each other about fishing, but we've yet to do it. He's trying to cut back on his medical practice, retire while he can."

"Where is he located?" It's hard listening to him talk when he's still holding and rubbing my hand with his thumb.

He chats on, paying little attention to my comments. He leans back in his chair, taking his hand with him. "I had a lot of clients like that. Buy a place, move down here and have a heart attack on the golf course." He snaps his fingers. "They're gone." Charles finishes his coffee, stands and puts his chair back against the wall. "I have to run. I'll make a list of health insurance companies for you to look over and the address of Hank's office." He was listening. "I'll see you later when I bring over some vegetables."

"I'm driving to town. If I'm not here, just leave them on the back porch. I don't think anyone will bother them there." I wave him off.

In spite of the fact Kat said no gifts, I'm getting her one. I drive into town to Bridges Books. The store is located on the waterfront looking over a creek and Sugarloaf Island, a small island, made larger by the spoils from dredging the port's deeper channel. It separates the creek from the Intracoastal Waterway, protecting the backside of the businesses from violent storms and offers a small hard packed beach for those with a small boat and the inclination to get there. Danny keeps rocking chairs on his porch for husbands to sit in while their wives browse. One man tips his hat and another nods as I pass through their conversation.

Danny glances up from behind his computer screen and smiles, "Welcome, stranger." He slides from behind his desk and meets me at the coffee carafes. He usually has three flavors. Today I fill a mug with hazelnut decaf, add skim milk, artificial sweetener and a sprinkle of cinnamon.

"*Mmm*, good." Although it's my third cup, Danny's coffee hits the spot. "I'm looking for a gift. I'd like something for a woman I just met. She plays a lot of bridge or -- maybe a nice journal. What do you have?"

He tops off his own mug with Killer Mean-Joe Brew and leads me to the back corner.

"I met her a few weeks ago at the library. She went out of her way to make me feel welcome and we hit it off. I think we'll be good friends." I hope he realizes I wasn't waiting for a phone call from him. "I've been busy. I'm taking a computer class at the college, still working at Help & Hands and I joined an Investment Club."

He says, "I liked it better when I was your only friend. I hate sharing you."

"Danny, I need you to understand this. I'm not yours to share. I thought I made it clear the other night."

He notices my tone and changes the subject to something safer. "Your book came in, Pat Conroy's." The phone rings.

"I'll get it." Nancy runs out of the stock room and picks up the receiver. "Oh, hi. No, now's not a good time. No, I haven't had a chance to talk with him yet." Long pause. "Is it really important?" Another pause. "Will I see you tonight?"

We hate to eavesdrop, but her conversation is so full of emotion, it flows to our section of the store.

"All right. Goodbye." She hangs up and sighs.

76

Begin Again, Quinn

Danny shrugs his shoulders, "Guess the Bridges siblings are striking out in the love category. I'll go see what we're supposed to talk about. If you need help, let me know." He retreats following Nancy into the storeroom.

I pick through the shelves and tables of gifts and find a purple, leather-bound, blank-paged book embossed with irises. I pick up two, one for Kat and one for myself with a couple of extra filler pads.

As I head back up to the checkout counter, Danny's voice explodes from the storeroom. "No, if you want another house, I'll buy you out. I'm not selling my home!" He storms out the back door as Nancy glances toward me.

She comes to the register and smiles meekly. "Would you like those wrapped?"

"Yes, but only one. The other is for me." She points to three kinds of paper.

"I like the one with balloons. Let me get a card too. Before I forget, Danny mentioned you have a book for me."

When I return she's wrapped the gift and stuck a bow in the corner. She drops everything into a newsprint-decorated sack and hands it to me when I pay.

"It's none of my business, but Danny seemed upset." Now I feel like Jessica Fletcher, sticking my nose where it doesn't belong. "I'm sure it wasn't a good time. I'd just told him something he didn't want to hear." I'm trying to smooth over his outburst and my curiosity, but it doesn't work. I'll have to watch a few more episodes and learn Jessica's questioning technique. The "Murder She Wrote" sleuthstress made it look easy.

Nancy never talked much to me when she was a child. She isn't sharing anything now. She stares back at me until I leave the store.

Since Grier and I began walking every morning, I've changed my diet. My old clothes are looser. As I browse the women's section of Goodwill, I spy Daphne George at the jewelry counter across the aisle. I duck behind a clothes rack as she asks the clerk to show her something under the glass.

After the way she treated me at her house, my avoidance is automatic. She fingers a watch, a necklace and a ring. When the clerk turns her head to wait on another customer, Daphne tucks something in her purse. She picks up her colorful cane and leans on it as she turns.

I'm dumbfounded. This deliberate theft irks me enough to confront her. When I step in her path, she glares at me.

"You didn't pay for that." My Daddy, not to mention the Ten Commandments, is backing me up.

She's defiant. "What? You must be mistaken." She stamps her cane trying to get me to step aside.

I hold my ground.

"Oh, yes," she turns, "I forgot," and tosses the necklace back on the counter, catching the clerk's eye. "I changed my mind. It's too cheap looking." She tugs at her over-blouse and waddles away, swinging her cane like a metal detector as she goes.

As I drive home, the revelations of the day claw at my mind. The stack of unread paperback mysteries doesn't interest me. I'm drawn to my backyard to sit and watch the boats on the waterway. When I step out on the back porch heading for my chair in the shade, I stumble over an old washtub of freshly picked vegetables, a jar of pickles and an envelope with names of health insurance companies.

###

Gerald Gillikin shuffles into his workshop. Since his wife's death eighteen months earlier, he hasn't felt like carving. At one time, his decoys won prizes in the local competitions. He doesn't remember when he last entered a contest. That's part of his problem. He can't remember things at all any more. If he sees food in the refrigerator, he eats it, but can't tell you when he ate last. His son is busy with work or the grandchildren. His daughter lives in the western part of the state. It seems like she was just here.

His thin pajamas hang on his body; his feet slide in a pair of scuffed leather slippers. Now where is the ruddy duck? It seems like a recent project but in fact, it's been months since he turned on the lights in his workshop. His hands shake visibly as he searches among the broken heads and bodies of carving rejects. Never feeling the pain, he nicks his palm on a knife. Blood drips slowly from his hand.

A recent storm blew a tree against the building, crumbling one corner. Water drips down the frame and puddles across the floor. Power equipment cords, some frayed, run along the concrete pad. It's almost as if someone laid them in the puddle. Gerald's hand automatically reaches for the power switch. There's a loud pop and the lights go off.

They'll find the body Sunday when his son comes to visit and bring him lunch.

NINE

Later the next day, I'm sitting on the front porch when I hear Charles' back door slam. The vegetables are cooked or in the refrigerator and I haven't thanked him. He usually walks in the evening so I round my porch and holler. "Charles, would you like some company on your walk this evening? I have investment questions."

He nods.

"Let me get my notepad." I run in the front door and lock it, grabbing up my keys, pad and pen.

"Been doing your homework?" Charles walked around his fence and now leans on my front stoop. "Jump in. What's the first question?"

"Well first, I want to thank you for the garden bounty I found on my back steps."

"You're welcome. I never grew anything before I retired. I'm getting the hang of the planting, waiting, watering and weeding. It gives me something to think about every year, you know browsing seed catalogs and getting the ground ready." For a man who hasn't said more than a few gruff words to me the past several months he sure opened up lately. "There will be more before the summer is out. Now what kinds of questions do you have?"

"I don't understand the difference between an annuity and a mutual fund. Can you explain that?"

"You've been studying." We head up the street as he educates me. "A mutual fund is a collection of stocks or bonds, managed by a firm. They buy and sell the securities on your behalf. You receive the dividends, interest and capital gains or they reinvest to buy more shares. You pay taxes on them, unless they're tax-exempt. There's no guarantee on the value of principle or return." He rambles on like he's explained it many times. "An annuity is tax-deferred. The earnings aren't taxed until you withdraw them. It can be mutual funds or similar to a bank CD, a certificate of deposit, an insured principle and return. Understand the difference between tax-free and tax-deferred?"

"Yep, I got it," I say.

"There are usually higher fees and penalties for an annuity. Both Uncle Sam and the insurance company have their penalties, taxes and surrender charges if you don't abide by the contract. Understand?" He stops walking.

"I think I do, but if you die, what happens, or what happens if you are receiving payments, not just interest, but interest and principle and you die?"

He considers the question, "The easy answer is if you die before you start distributions, the annuity pays out like a life insurance policy to your heirs."

"Okay and the long answer?" I prompt him.

"The long answer is when you start receiving payments, you select from a list of options. One is guaranteed income for life." He holds his back like it's bothering him, but doesn't mention it as we walk. "Another might be a guaranteed payout for so many years, like five, ten, or twenty years. Some have survivor benefits for a spouse. It's a gamble unless you know when you'll die."

"So if I were to say, pay me for life and then I die, there is no survivor benefit."

He answers, "For the most part, yes. If you chose lifetime benefits with no survivor benefit, your monthly income is higher."

"How do they figure that?"

He grabs my hand as he walks. "Boy, you ask hard questions." He pats my hand. "We call them actuarial tables. All insurance companies have them." He's careful with his words.

"These tables are the same for all companies?"

"Usually. Some companies vary a bit, but generally, they all use similar figures. Now you know more than eighty percent of the people out there," he chuckles. "Most financial advisors are licensed to sell anything, stocks, bonds, mutual funds or annuities. I was one of those. The problem is some insurance agents only sell annuities or life insurance. That product may not be what you need, but it's all they sell. It's a tough business, no matter on which side of the desk you're sitting. Glad I retired when I did."

I enjoy listening to his voice. It's easy to understand why he was successful. "Do you know anything about reverse mortgages?"

"Banks, mortgage companies and insurance companies sell them. I even saw an 800-number on television the other night." He strokes his chin with his free hand. "I know one case of a woman selling her house in France, I think, as a reverse mortgage, who outlived the buyer. I think she was over a hundred when she died. She received income from the buyer's estate for the rest of her life. It was in the paper a few years back. The reverse mortgage paid for her house several times over. She beat the odds. It's supposed to be a win-win situation for the bank or insurance company and the retirees needing income but not ready to move out of their house. I don't know much more. Why are you interested in reverse mortgages? You just bought your house."

"Yep, but I know of someone who did the reverse mortgage thing and both he and his wife died. It just doesn't seem right the company would get the house so soon and not have to pay more to their survivors."

"That's a job for the paper-pushers. You needn't get involved with that. These things are monitored."

He's still holding my hand. "No more questions?"

I shake my head and we go a several more blocks before we head back. He lets go of my hand when we stop at my porch.

Begin Again, Quinn

"Good night. I've enjoyed our walk, Quinn. Maybe we can do it again." He turns and walks to his own home.

I'm too stunned to say anything back.

TEN

The next week, I arrive early for the Country Club luncheon and park my car in a distant shady space. The car will be cooler and I'll burn off a few more calories. Asking my way around, I find some of the group on the last hole where Eleanor's lining up her final shot. A basket of empty water bottles hangs from the rear of the golf cart.

"Is it a hot day or what?" Kat fans herself as she empties another bottle and tosses it into the basket.

"*Shhh*, be quiet, Katherine. If I miss this putt, you will be buying the drinks." Eleanor crouches on the green studying her shot, stands, moves easily back to the cart and changes her putter.

Kat smiles smugly. I don't see Grier, but Tricia waves and tiptoes over.

"The others already left. We're finishing up." Holding her monogrammed water bottle cooler in one hand, she shades her face with the other. She tips the bottle up, finishing her drink and smiles. "I did pretty well myself today, third best score behind these two." She clips the bottle onto her golf bag.

"Yes!" Both hands in the air, Eleanor urges the white ball into the hole. "All right ladies, I'm buying." Kat goes with Eleanor to return the cart to the pro-shop, while Tricia and I hurry into the air conditioned clubhouse. The earlier arrivals secured a table and decorated it with balloons, ribbons and party trinkets. Kat is like a child when she sees the table. She grabs up a cone hat and tucks the elastic beneath her chin. "You shouldn't have. This is so special, you guys went all out." The peppermint striped cap rests easily on top of her curls.

She seats herself amid friends and takes a big gulp of water from her glass. Some of us join in her fun, donning our own hats. Daphne looks over my head as if I'm not here. An eager server presents herself, order pad in hand.

"Hi, my name is Brandi. I'll be your server today."

Kat places her drink order. "I'd like something tall and cold. What do you have?"

Brandi looks like a red-haired Barbie doll wearing a tuxedo shirt, black cummerbund and dress slacks, but her Down-east brogue slips into her conversation. "We have Bloody Marys on special, sounds like just the thing for you, honey."

"I'll have a gin and tonic." Eleanor straightens in her chair to close the blinds striping sunlight across her face. "I haven't played this well since I graduated from nursing school. They warn about playing when it's so hot."

"I didn't know you were a nurse," I say.

"Yes," she grins, "me and the entire senior class met my husband in nursing school. Oh, I shouldn't have said that. It was mean." There's a glint in her eye. "The good doctor had a fondness for nurses. I was flattered when he asked me out, but I said no. Then he seriously pursued me, until I let him catch me." She smiles, sharing her story.

Kat changes her order, "On second thought, make me two Bloody Marys." She winks at the young woman who adjusts the order. Kat watches her go, licking her lips. She takes another swallow of water. "I want everyone to order anything you want from the menu. This is my day, so no arguing about who's paying. Oh, but Eleanor is buying the drinks!"

"*Ha*," Eleanor comments smugly, having won the match.

The server returns. "Here you go, ladies. I'm sorry about the wait. We're a person short today. I think I have everyone's right." She dispenses the drinks including both of Kat's. "Enjoy."

"What's on special today?" Grier asks.

"We have shrimp salad on a croissant with a choice of slaw, potato salad or fruit cup," Brandi replies.

"Oh, that sounds good," says Grier.

"Would you like to order now or should I give you more time?"

"Give us a minute. We haven't all decided." Eleanor dismisses the young woman. She eyes Kat. "Careful dear, you shouldn't drink so fast.

Grier and Tricia sip margaritas. I never liked the taste of alcohol, but my ginger ale and orange juice hits the spot.

"Alice, tell us about your house-hunting. Have you found anything interesting?" Daphne, the group gossip, wants to get the information first hand.

Alice puts her wine aside. With an encouraging nod from her realtor, she explains, "At first I wanted to be on the beach like you, Eleanor, but I'm afraid of the hurricanes. We found a townhouse. I won't have high water. It was an old family estate. Now it's sub-divided into a retirement community." Alice's jacket to her pale blue three-piece suit hangs on the back of her chair. "The townhouse I want is all on one level with a gas log fireplace, two bedrooms and two baths. I love the kitchen. There's an island with a tiny sink in it, lots of cabinet space, a private courtyard and garden."

"I see. Well, I suppose if you can't be on the beach, at least you can see water. I've always said if you are going to live in this county you must be on the water." Daphne shifts in her chair for emphasis. Her printed dress covers the tops of her arms and hides her bulk in a swirl of polyester color. She wears enough 'bling' on her ears to blind a deer in the dark.

Alice blinks, trying to decide if Daphne was making a snide remark or a casual comment. She takes another sip of her wine then continues, "I'm planning on replacing the carpeting. The previous owner had a dog, if you know what I mean." She lowers her voice, "I think it's why it hasn't sold.

Begin Again, Quinn

We made an offer, pending my home sale. I don't want to get my hopes up, but I already think of it as mine. Tricia's been such a great help." Alice beams with pleasure. "It's my first major purchase since Ken's death."

Kat drains the first glass and takes a bite of the celery stalk. "*Mmm*, that hit the spot." She glances at Eleanor. "I promise to drink this next one slower. When can we see it?"

"I think we better wait until I sell mine. I got a call from Lloyd Batts the other day. He calls me all the time wanting referrals for his insurance business." She makes a face and takes another sip of wine.

"I hate to break it to you, but both our least favorite people are here." Tricia nods over to the bar and nudges me. "The wiry-haired, ham-faced one at this end of the bar is Lloyd Batts. You'd think he'd know by now polyester suits went out with eight-track tapes. The cute butt fellow at the other end is Kat's nephew, Lee Kelson. He looks like a banker, even in this weather, long sleeves, tie-bar and expensive suit. At least he dresses for success."

We turn towards the bar as Lee steps down from his perch and walks toward an attractive woman. He guides her back to the other end of the dining room. Planters, white Doric columns and gauzy curtains divide the dining room into sections.

Tricia continues, "I have to say I like what Lee did with his new project, Sea Grove. It's all brick, very high end condominiums. The fountains and landscaping are gorgeous. Nice touches, little twinkling lights on the surrounding trees and courtyard at night." Tricia stops and stares at Kat. "Girl, are you still hot? You're glowing."

Kat barely glances to the bar. "What's wrong with me? I guess I overheated with the excitement of my party. My skin feels prickly." She takes another gulp of her cold drink and unbuttons her top button. "Would you look at my hands? They're swelling up." She gasps, "Oh no, I can't brea…." As Kat's head falls to the side, Eleanor and Alice reach out to catch her.

"Good Lord, someone call 911. Katherine," Eleanor, always in charge, calls out, "Can you hear me?" She grabs Kat's purse, pulls out an Epipen, cracks off the cap. She plunges the point into Kat's thigh. "Come on, girl. Come back to us."

Tricia reaches for her cell phone.

Eleanor places the used Epipen in her pocket. "I can't believe I sat here and didn't recognize the symptoms."

Daphne says, "Is she breathing? Let me see." She lunges up, taking part of the tablecloth with her.

Eleanor's fingers feel beneath Kat's collar. Kat gasps and pulls her head back. Her eyes roll to the side. By this time, Brandi, our waitress, has pulled the restaurant manager to our table.

Eleanor tells her, "It's an allergic reaction."

The manager calls two wait staff over. Only the closest tables note a problem as the restaurant employees carry Kat, using her chair as a make-shift stretcher, to the front door of the restaurant.

When the ambulance arrives, Eleanor tells the EMTs about the possible clam allergy and shows them the empty epinephrine dispenser. One ambulance worker takes Kat's vitals while another gathers medical information. Settling the bill, we gather Kat's purse and our own belongings, leaving the empty party table as a sad reminder. This could have been her last birthday.

Across the room, Lee Kelson barely glances at the disturbance at our end of the restaurant. I can't see Lloyd Batts anywhere. Grier and I pick up our presents and hurry to my car. We follow the ambulance to the hospital.

Grier and I sit together in the chilled waiting room. "I feel like a mule with a burr under my blanket." I can't help but ask, "Did everyone in the investment club know about Kat's allergy to clams?"

Grier squints at the ceiling remembering, "Yes. I seem to recall a mild episode years ago when we were out eating somewhere. She's been so careful." Her brows furrow. "I'm glad Eleanor recognized the symptoms and grabbed that Epipen." Grier is wringing her hands.

I grab them and tell her my thoughts. "Maybe Danny's right." I say, "Maybe someone's killing people, like widows and widowers like the women in this club. Except for you and Daphne, everyone else is single in the group, right?"

"What? You think this was intentional. How does an allergic reaction relate to murder?" Grier's eyes widen. "Oh, you think someone wanted to kill Kat!"

"It could be someone in the investment club. Do you think the investment pool is large enough to kill for?"

"Gosh, how do you come up with these ideas?" Grier squeezes my hands.

"Well, since I'm a member of this group, of a certain age and marital status, I need to know these things. What I'm trying to decide is how this is related. Tricia says money's always a good motive. Speaking of which, where is she?" I turn around in my chair.

Grier pulls me around. "She's over there."

Through the plate glass window, we see Tricia talking excitedly on her cell phone and waving her hand. Grier shrugs her shoulders. "Whoever she's talking to is getting an ear full. I wouldn't want to be on the receiving end of that conversation."

Eleanor loses her patience and stands, "That's it, enough waiting." She walks over to a woman at the registration desk.

"Can I help you?" A chubby receptionist, holding a clipboard, leans away from the counter at Eleanor's approach.

"Yes, I came in with a friend two hours ago. Could I speak with the doctor about her condition?"

"Are you family? We aren't allowed to give out information except to family until she's admitted." Her strained voice rises.

Eleanor grabs the woman's hand and steps towards her. "Get me your supervisor immediately, dear. I won't be put off another minute."

A thin, frizzy-haired woman, wearing a brown cardigan, comes to the desk. They speak for a few minutes. Eleanor takes notes.

After thanking the supervisor, she returns. "It *was* an allergic reaction. I knew it, but she has a heart condition too. Did you know that?"

"What did you say?" Grier's ears prick up like a cat hearing a whirring can opener. "I never knew anything about a heart problem."

"They've stabilized her and will be moving her up to a room this evening. She's not to have visitors until tomorrow. Her personal physician happened to be in the hospital when it was called in."

Daphne snorts. "She knows she's allergic and a bad heart, to boot. She shouldn't have played golf on a day like this. If we can't see her, I'm going home." She pushes herself up from the chair and plants her cane as she reaches down for her purse. "No sense wasting time here." She tromps off.

Eleanor raises an eyebrow. "Pure luck she started carrying an Epipen. If I hadn't found it, she'd be dead!"

"Eleanor," Grier comforts her friend, "you saved her life."

Eleanor shakes off Grier's words, "Any one of you would have done the same thing." She checks her notes, "Guess that's about it. We may as well go home and come back in the morning."

I'm relieved. "Can I drop you back to the club, Cuz? I want to go back and talk to Brandi."

"Yeah, I need to pick up my car. Now you got me thinking. I may need to clue Sam in, if your suspicions are right."

Driving back to the country club, I say, "Someone could have switched the drinks or put something in hers."

"It could just be a mistake."

I'm thinking about who had access to Kat's drinks during the day. "I remember all those empty water bottles in the golf cart. Did she drink several bottles of water while you played golf? Something could have been in the bottled water, but it didn't faze the rest of you."

"Tricia brought the water today. Mine tasted fine."

We drive to the clubhouse, talk with Brandi and the restaurant manager. We plan to meet for our morning walk as usual before going to the hospital.

ELEVEN

The following morning, I drive over to pick up Grier and her dog for our walk. She motions me inside. I watch husband and wife square off like fencing competitors.

"Come on, give me a break. The primary crimes in this county are break-ins and DWIs. The few murders we have in the area are from a bad drug deal or sometimes when a spouse kills a partner. Quit with the television murder mystery stuff." He shakes out his morning paper.

Grier stomps her foot with both hands on her hips.

He lowers his paper again. "Okay, Grier, let me get this straight. You believe someone poisoned your friend, Katherine Knowles, at the country club, with a tainted Bloody Mary. It sounds more like the butler, with the candlestick, in the library. I've never heard of anyone who kills with clam juice. If that is what it was, whether in the water bottle or Bloody Mary. Clams aren't your ordinary garden-variety poison."

Grier looks at me for backup, but I'm staying out of this. I want to hear a professional's opinion.

She licks her lip. "I tasted the juice when we went back to the club. It was definitely tomato. The only way her drink could have clam juice in it was if someone replaced the regular stuff -- to kill Kat. Everyone in the Investment Club knows she's allergic to clams." Grier leans over the breakfast table and goes head to head with her husband.

Sam stares up at his wife with a sweet smile on his face. With a bustle and ringlets of curls, she'd make a smoldering Scarlett O'Hara, but in a fluorescent orange halter-top and skin-tight exercise shorts, Sam can't take her seriously.

"First, no restaurant is going to 'fess up to using the wrong juice and they probably threw it out as soon as Katherine got sick. Second, if it was a joke, who would admit it now? There must have been a couple hundred people there between the golfers and weekday lunches they normally serve." Sam shakes his head and sits back, finishing the sports section of the Raleigh paper. He folds the paper for his crossword puzzle and pulls out his pen. End of discussion.

Grier growls while she clears the table of breakfast dishes. Sam ignores her unhappy noises. "I'm taking the dog for his walk." She jingles the leash by the door and the big dog grunts up from his cool spot on the air-conditioning vent.

"Quinn, I tried, but he's not buying the murder attempt. Are you ready?" We head for the door. "You knew who the killer was in Margaret Maron's last book. You notice things most people," she glares at Sam, "overlook. Let's go."

In the car, she pushes the passenger seat back into its deepest position, pulls her feet up on the seat and tugs Mojo inside. He circles and lies down with a soft woof. Grier gingerly rests a leg over the big dog while keeping her other foot tucked in the seat. She finds a piece of bubble gum in of her fanny pack, unwraps it and pops it into her mouth. Since I'm driving today, my choice for the morning walk is an older section of town. By the time we reach the visitor parking lot, her pink gum is a juicy gob. She begins to blow a bubble. Too bad the gum isn't orange to match the rest of her outfit.

We walk from the Visitor Center toward the old beach bridge cutoff. The houses overlook Bogue Sound. Dark green awnings shade their southern exposures. Shutters hug each window. Geraniums and vincas tumble from flower boxes in pretty postcard pictures. Crepe myrtles and ivy bank the sidewalks in shady spots. Occasionally the smell of boxwoods reaches my nose. Honeysuckle and jasmine climb lattice screening.

While the sea breeze blows fragrance across our path, unpleasant thoughts invade my mind. "I believe someone tried to kill Kat." I say.

Grier chews the wad over to the side of her mouth. She yanks Mojo's leash as he wanders too far into a yard. "This sounds like a whodunit. *Pop.*" A small bubble explodes between her lips. She pulls it back in her mouth with her tongue and chomps on it again. "You think someone in the club is killing off the members so she can get at the investment pool? Or -- do you think Kat's nephew is trying to kill everyone so he can get to the money? Why would he want to kill Kat?" She starts to blow a bigger one this time.

"If Kat were to die he'd inherit everything she has. Forget the investment pool. That would go to the rest of the club. Tricia and I talked about him the other day."

"Kat has a good share of the pool," Grier says.

"Tricia mentioned real estate and money in the investment pool are good motives." It's hard to concentrate on our conversation while my cousin plays with a sheet of bubble gum plastered across her face. "Is there any evidence Margaret Byrd was pushed down those steps behind her home?"

"Oh, my God. I forgot about Birdie." Grier strings the gum out and then rolls it up into her mouth again. "I'm sorry. I chew bubble gum when I get upset."

"Well, she was a member of the club, too." I mention my growing basket of accidental deaths. When I get home, maybe I'll throw them all in the trash. "By the way, you have a piece here," I point to my face and she rescues the sticky pink off her cheek.

Grier turns the dog up the old bridge road and leans against the guardrail. I join her. We watch a sailboat running with the tide glide up the waterway.

"Maybe it's a coincidence." She wipes her bangs up into her hat. "I just finished a book last night on synchronicity. The main theory is similar things occur, with no reason, at the same time." She frowns, staring down at the ground. "Let's say you broke your hip and on the evening news, there's a report about women breaking their hips. That's synchronicity."

"I'd like to believe that."

Begin Again, Quinn

Grier grimaces. "I don't want to think about a murderer in the group. Let's hope it is coincidence."

"The Bible says there are times for living and times for dying." My mind reaches back to my Sunday school days. "This is the time we lose friends and family, unfortunately."

The tall sloop slides under the bridge while I wait for her to confirm my thoughts.

She pokes my elbow. "Cuz, maybe this is just like when we were girls. While we sipped our cherry Cokes at the drug store, we turned ordinary people into killers as we watched them buy aspirin or talk to the pharmacist."

She finally wads the ball of gum back into its wrapper. She stuffs it back into the bag and tugs at the leash, heading back the way we came. "Maybe Sam's right. We're letting our imagination get the best of us." She washes her hands of the bubblegum and the murder theory, on a moist towelette pulled from her bottomless fanny pack.

I count on my fingers, "Yeah, but I'm single, wealthy, old," I cringe, "and a member of the Investment Club. I'm keeping my options open."

"Got it bad, don't you?" She laughs.

We head back up the sidewalk. I take her home and then drive home to shower and change. Before I meet her at the hospital, I clip a bundle of Japanese irises to take.

A dozen friends line the hallway outside Kat's room. We take turns going in to see her. While Grier and I are in Kat's room, the phone rings. I try not to listen as I fill a water pitcher for the flowers.

A voice comes through the telephone receiver, "Aunt Katherine, how are you doing? I just found out about your accident."

He talks so loud Kat has to hold the receiver away from her ear. I want to grab the phone and tell him she's not deaf. She has a heart condition and a near fatal allergic reaction.

His voice continues to spout. "What can I do for you? Would you like to come stay a while with Ginger and me?"

"Thank you but no, Lee."

"Well, can I at least take you home when the doctor says you can leave? How about I arrange for someone to stay with you?" He doesn't wait for her answer. "We've talked about all this before. You may need to reconsider your options, you know, have someone to make certain you take your medicines and help you get around."

Kat nods. "Lee, I've told you before I don't want anything to change. I'm not ready for the nursing home. I can handle my own finances and deal with daily living. I don't know when I can go home. My friends are here now. One will pick me up and take me home. A couple more will be dropping in bringing food after I'm settled. I'll let you know when I'm ready for company." It's obvious she doesn't want her nephew to visit. Kat changes the subject. "How are Ginger and Mildred, her mother?"

Grier and I turn politely and look out the window. Across the road, the Carteret Community College faces Bogue Sound. The island across the sound simmers in the morning sun. I say a silent prayer for whoever thought of building a hospital with this view. Most hospitals look out at brick buildings and asphalt parking lots.

Kat shakes her head as she holds the receiver away and flinches.

"Listen, that little money problem I had, well it's been taken care of for now. I appreciate your patience, *ha-ha*. I haven't upset you, have I? Forgive me, Aunt Katherine? I have your best interest at heart."

"Yes, Lee, " she assures him. "Just a minute, Lee." Kat interrupts. "Someone's knocking on the door. Yes, come in."

Tricia sticks her head in the room. "Your doctor's coming."

Begin Again, Quinn

"I have to hang up. Give my love to Ginger, dear." Kat pushes the handset back on her bedside table. "*Whoosh*," she makes a sound like a deflating balloon. "He can be so irritating."

The nurse shoos us out as Kat's doctor slides in between us. We hug the corridor wall, avoiding carts, patients with walkers pulling IVs and wheelchairs.

Tricia glances at her watch, "Well, I have to be going. She looks fine, don't you think? For a person whose heart stopped beating, she looks good. Eleanor, you have fast reflexes."

Eleanor presses back against the wall, crossing her hands above her elbows. "I did what I was trained to do." She pulls at her collar, allowing the short strand of gray pearls to drop onto her neck. "If she has to stay another day, I'm bringing her a nightgown. Those hospital gowns are appalling." She dismisses Tricia, who departs through a stairway door. "Kat looks pitiful without her glasses, with all those wires and tubes. They're being very careful with her and I'm glad. I think insurance companies rush patients out of the hospital too quickly." Eleanor rarely misses anything. "Were those flowers from your garden, Quinn? They're lovely and smell so nice."

"Yes, the final blooms. I'm glad I could bring them."

Kat's young doctor leaves. As he walks up the hall, remaining friends flow back into the private room.

"Well, they're going to keep me another night. Clam juice strikes again. Would you believe it? I've no idea how that happened. Did anyone else taste it in your drink?

"No? *Humph*." She shrugs. "I guess from now on I bring my own water if we go out. They want to be sure all this mess is out of my system and I'm neutralized!" She counts heads, "Well, I feel up to it. Who can stay and play bridge?"

In unison, we exclaim, "Kat!" As the hour goes by, someone promises to visit later and bring a deck of cards.

Karen Dodd

I return home to read my newspaper. Instead of throwing out my clippings, I find another accidental death. I reach for my scissors and after trimming off the edges, allow the latest accidental death notice to float down into the basket.

"Beloved Teacher Found Dead

A visiting nurse found seventy-eight year old Agatha Adamms dead in her Beaufort home Monday evening. Friends of the woman tell the police she was suffering from depression since her sister's death in January of this year. Initial conclusions indicate her taking her sister's medicine by mistake. The two retired schoolteachers lived in their family home on North River. Parents, Thomas and Olive Adamms and sister, Alice Adamms, predeceased her.

Adamms graduated from Women's College in Greensboro and served as class historian for the past fifty years. She was a member of the First Baptist Church of Beaufort, the Beaufort Women's Club and a charter member of the County Historical Society where she volunteered as secretary for eighteen years.

"She taught first grade for thirty-three years at Beaufort Elementary School," former principal, Thomas Lewis, said. "She was a wonderful teacher. Her former students visited during their college breaks and class reunions. We will miss her."

A memorial service will be held on Friday at 3:00 at the First Baptist Church of Beaufort. In lieu of flowers, friends are urged to contribute to the Beaufort Historical Society's Agatha Adamms' Costume Benefit Fund."

###

He amazes himself with his power over life and death. If it lines his pockets, so be it. Miss Adamms took so many pills. She confessed she sometimes confused her sister's pills with her own, a fatal mistake.

Begin Again, Quinn

TWELVE

The summer's heat forces us to walk earlier each morning. Getting back from my walk, I take a pitcher of iced tea and two glasses to the fence. Charles smiles as he tosses down his hoe and comes over. As dirt mixes with the sweat on his face, he pulls a dishtowel from his back pocket and wipes his face and hands.

"Good morning, neighbor."

"Hello, Charles, I thought you'd like something cool to drink." I pour him a tall glass.

He takes several long swallows. "Nectar from the gods. I can't keep ahead of the weeds. No sooner do I finish one row, I look back and they are sprouting again."

"You're feeding them too well."

"Yeah, maybe so."

He drains his glass. "Thank you." He places the glass on a fence post and rests his hands between the pickets of the fence. "I've been meaning to tell you," he removes his hat and wipes out the headband with the towel, "after our talk about my brother and his family the other day, I called him."

"Wonderful, I'm glad I prodded you. What have you missed?"

"I'm a great-uncle -- again. He said they'd come down for a visit. I'd like you to be a part of our get-together since you suggested I call. We can all do something together. Maybe go out to eat or drive up to New Bern or Oriental," he hesitates. "If you want to."

"Sounds like fun. When are they coming?" I wonder if he's being neighborly or if there's more to his suggestion. "I'm finishing up my class at the community college in three weeks and I'll have lots of free time."

"They'll be here the week before Labor Day. Is that good for you?" He holds his glass out for another fill-up.

"I don't have anything planned. I'll put it on my calendar." I'm delighted.

"Do you know that man over there in the blue car?" Charles points to the faded sedan parked across the street. "He pulled up a moment ago and is watching us."

Turning to look over my shoulder, I recognize the car. My face warms in a flash of anger. "I hate to admit it, but he used to be my husband. Since he found out I have some money, he's come around pestering me. I called the police about him last time."

"Well, I'll see if I can have a word with him."

"No, Charles. Please, I'm sure he'll go away."

Charles stuffs his towel back in his pocket and straightens to walk across the yard to his gate. "I'll see what he wants."

I hear the engine cough and Matt plows away from the curb. Charles stares at the car a moment longer. He takes his top pocket pen and writes the license plate down on his palm as he walks back to me. "Give the police this license number when you talk with them." I memorize the letters written on his hand.

"Thank you Charles. I learned to tell people about his abuse or intimidation in the classes I went to after I moved here. Having a witness, like yourself, is good when I report him again. I may take out a new restraining order."

"You be careful."

We finish our tea and after a few awkward moments, I gather the glasses and return to the house. I immediately go to my calendar and enter a note on the week Charles' brother might come. Picking up the phone, I call Sam.

He's out, but they take my message. The desk officer is polite.

The Golden Girls Investment Club meets at my house in the morning. I mop the bathroom and kitchen floors. Grier told me to fix light finger foods. I can't decide between oatmeal raisin or chocolate chip cookies, so I bake both.

Sam calls when he returns to his office. "I'm sorry I'm getting back to you so late. Is your husband bothering you again?"

"My ex-husband and I'm afraid so." I explain what happened.

"Threats, stalking and physical assault are all against the law in North Carolina. Do you want to take out a warrant for his arrest?"

"I wish he would just go away, but it looks like I need to do more, doesn't it?"

"It sounds like the man is running a fine line here. I'll bring him in for a talk. If he doesn't toe the line, he faces arrest."

"Oh Sam, would you?" I reach for the piece of paper where I wrote down the numbers. "I copied down his license plate. Let me give it to you."

He takes the information. After all the cleaning and baking, I shower. The phone rings as I finish dressing. The caller ID display indicates an unknown number. Avoiding the annoying rings, I walk outside to turn on my lawn sprinklers delaying my return to the house. Eventually, the ringing stops.

A fine spray catches me as I walk around the yard. The tiny azalea bushes I've nurtured show a healthy growth and I'm please with the new sprouts of foxglove and lantana. Daddy used to hang the garden hose over the clothesline on sweltering days. The mist on my face brings back those memories. Other days I clipped sheets to the clothesline to make a dollhouse or Indian Teepee. I wonder where all the clotheslines went.

Mama and her clothespin bag were almost daily sights when I was a girl. The sheets smelled so good when she made the beds. Mama had a good recipe for blueberry torte. I may as well make something cool for the club members. I satisfy my dieter guilt by reminding myself blueberries are one of the healthiest foods.

With the torte chilling in my refrigerator, I kick off my shoes to prop my feet up on an old trunk. Violet Rosenberg, the retired art professor in Raleigh, who left me her furniture and car, fell in her bathroom breaking her hip. She never recovered after she went to the nursing home. "Remember the sparrow…" Little prayers pop in my head when I count my blessings.

The sun leaves the sky. I glance about the Carolina room, taking a deep satisfied breath. I keep a stack of books in a basket, so I pick up the top one, read until I'm sleepy.

Karen Dodd

###

Earlier than expected the next morning, I hear a call. *"YOO-HOO."* Grier tugs at the front screen.

I go out and unlock the door as she pushes her way into the house. "Taking precautions, are we? Sam told me you called. He'll take care of it." She pats my shoulder and drops her purse on the kitchen counter. *"Mmm.* The house smells wonderful. I thought I'd come early and help. What can I do?"

I slide a tray of cookies and a plate of vegetable munchies onto the counter. "Would you mind carrying the chairs from my bedroom and office out to the back room?" I pull out the drop- leaf table. "Here's a tablecloth and you can bring these trays for me."

"Everything looks so nice, Honey. You look special in your new duds." Grier recognizes my clothes.

"Thank you. There's a vase of flowers by the back door. Center them on the table, please." After spreading dairy topping over Mama's torte filling, I garnish the top with a few fresh blueberries.

"Here this can go out, too. I've made coffee and two pitchers of tea. Can you think of anything else?" I pull my apron over my head.

"Nope. Looks like you've done it all, honey child. Sit and catch your breath before people start coming." Grier straightens the forks and lines up the glasses on the side cabinet.

"There's someone at the door. I'll get it." Grier primps, then in character with her Southern lady's image walks casually to the door.

I check my face in the mirror over the couch and pull a few misplaced sprigs of hair into place. My new hairdresser showed me how to tousle it, even though I never tousled anything in my life.

Eleanor, carrying two designer bags, sashays toward me like a model on the runway. "One of the best things about this group is almost everyone is prompt." She fixes herself a cup of coffee and finds a chair at the corner of the room where she has a commanding view of my garden and other members as they arrive. "Lovely, Quinn. Everything looks lovely."

As the other women arrive, they admire the house and my summer garden. It's now in its wildflower bloom stage. My roses have climbed to the top of the trellis; daisies and poppies poke up around the fountain.

Alice marvels at my yard. "You did this all yourself? Have you ever thought of having a landscaping business? I'd love you to come see my little yard when I am settled. I can use a few tips."

Tricia Lewis comes up. "I can name a few contractors who would like you on their payroll." She seems to be mentally tallying the increase in property value.

Alice says, "Tricia, have you had any interest in my old house? Something happened yesterday. I have to tell someone about it before I go crazy."

We listen to Alice's report of her previous morning's encounter.

"I came down the stairs yesterday morning to drink my first cup of coffee. When I walked to the living room and pulled the drapery back, Lloyd Batts was parked in my driveway." She frowns describing what happened next. "He's like a bad penny," she mutters. "Anyway, as Lloyd picked up the morning paper, my past flooded back. Ken insisted on me cooking three meals a day for him and sometimes Lloyd came for lunch. When I opened the door, I said. 'What do you want?'

"'Is that any way to treat an old friend of the family, Alice?' He's such a bothersome man." She puts her hands on her hips and shakes her body imitating the man. "'Why are you selling this place?' He thumbed the front yard sign, while he strolled past me to the kitchen. Then he took a cup and poured himself *my* coffee. He said, 'I thought you liked it here. Ken bought this house for you eighteen years ago.'

"I told him, 'Ken didn't buy it for me. It was in the right neighborhood and it suited his image.'" Alice makes a prune face. "I thought of calling the police."

Tricia said, "Were you afraid?"

Alice shakes her head, "Not really, more uncomfortable than afraid. He pulled another cup from the cabinet. 'You take cream and sugar, don't you, Sweetheart?'"

"I told him I wasn't prepared for company and asked him to leave." She pounds her fist into her hand. "I never liked him before. I certainly didn't want to talk with him now."

Tricia interrupts, "He knows how to manipulate people."

"When I told him to leave, he laughed in my face. He said if I called the police, he'd explain he was visiting his partner's widow, who seemed to be having a mental breakdown."

Alice continues, "He's such a ridiculous sight. That belly sags over his belt. He's never without his cell phone, hanging on his belt like a six-shooter. He drank down my coffee in one long chug then grinned, one of those Jack Nicholson smiles." She shudders. "Well, I knocked the cup right out of his hand and walked to the front door and told him to get out."

"He said, 'No need to get upset, Alice.'" She puts her hands on her hips and waggles her head imitating Batts. "As he was walking out the door, he said, 'Oh, I almost forgot to tell you. You need to come by the office and change the beneficiary on your life insurance policy. You still have Ken listed.' I told him to drop the form in the mail." Alice flicks her hands, as if she's shaking off water. "With Ken gone, this group is my support group."

I say, "Then what did you do?" The retelling of her experience reminds me of my own past helplessness.

Alice puts a hand to her flushed face. She calms herself by fanning herself. "I went back to bed, I was so bothered, but I couldn't get back to sleep. I lay there thinking of Ken."

She takes my wrist and says, "My husband was a stickler about the car, taking it in for servicing. Ken often checked under the hood. He was proud of his car. How it ran into a ditch, I'll never understand.

Begin Again, Quinn

"The police thought the car hydroplaned. The roadside canal filled the car with water before the rescue squad could open the doors. I remember him worrying about something the week before he died, but he never shared with me."

As she composes herself, I hear another car door slam in front of the house. "Excuse me. I think someone's at the door." I walk up the hall and open my front door to the two stragglers.

"Welcome, Daphne, did you have a problem finding me?" I invite her and Pam Garner inside. "Come in. I think we're about to get started. Hello, Pam."

Pam Garner is a mouse of a woman who usually follows Daphne around. I've noticed her prim skirts and slacks with matching cardigans at previous meetings. Daphne's gaze wanders the hallway as she brushes by heading towards the sound of voices. Pam and I bring up the rear.

"I think your home is charming. I understand you did all this remodeling yourself?" This is the longest conversation Pam and I share.

Daphne overrides her comments. "I don't often come to this part of town. I didn't know which little narrow street to turn on. Isn't this a cute house? You've done the best with what you have, I suppose."

Pam shrugs her shoulders and follows her.

Dismissed by Daphne, I get myself a few carrots and cauliflower from the veggie tray, a small wedge of torte and pour a glass of unsweetened tea. Eleanor acknowledges the late arrivals. "Oh, good, everyone's here. We can get started if we can all find a seat."

When Daphne worms her way back to the refreshment table, Eleanor shakes her head and gets up to refill her own coffee cup. Hooking her cane on one arm, Daphne piles a plate high with cookies and torte, then backs up toward a window seat. I'm thinking garbage truck; she only needs the warning bells and lights. As she crouches to sit, she tilts her plate. An errant blueberry slides from the topping, rolls across the plate and bounces down the front of her silk blouse. The whipped topping-covered blueberry sluices down her front.

I hide a snicker behind my tea glass.

Daphne snorts her indignation at the delinquent berry. She reaches for a napkin to wipe her blouse, but only succeeds in smearing the juice.

Eleanor calls the group to order, "Shall we begin?" Soon attention turns to the reports of the day and suggestions for stock sales and purchases. As the business meeting closes, I notice Daphne gleaning once more from the desserts then she leaves without a glance back.

Pam waves at me. "Thank you. Everything was delicious. I enjoyed seeing your home."

As other guests depart, I escort them to the door. "I'm glad y'all came." I return to the back room to slt with the lingerers.

Alice comes up, "Slugs ate my irises this year. What do you use to keep them away?" It's good to see she recovered from the Lloyd description.

I chuckle. "My father would turn over in his grave. I feed them cheap beer. I put it in a shallow pie pan and they totter in every morning. I can't tell whether they drown or drink themselves to death!"

Alice shakes the wrinkles from her skirt. "Thank you for having us on such short notice. Everything was a delight. I love your home." She waves goodbye to the remaining guests.

Eleanor turns to me. "We'd like you to join us tomorrow night if you don't have other plans. Tricia, Grier and I plan on driving up to New Bern for dinner and a play." With Eleanor, it's more like a command than a request. I have no other plans and accept the invitation.

Begin Again, Quinn

"Were these your mother's? I sort of remember them." Grier rubs her finger along an engraved monogram on a silver serving spoon, polishes the last fork and closes the lid on my silver chest.

I take the wooden box my father made for my mother's silverware and shove it under the daybed in my guestroom. "Yep, I've never used them. This was a good excuse to get them out. It's nice to use all the fancy stuff." We return to the kitchen. "Here, take the rest of this torte for you and Sam. I've eaten enough."

I drop the remaining blueberry torte in a plastic tub and give Grier a bag of blueberries. "You were a big help. Thank you. Tomorrow night sounds like a dressy affair!" I pretend to throw a boa across my shoulder with a dramatic shrug. "Should I pick you up tomorrow morning for our downtown walk?"

"No, I'll meet you there. I'll have to carry weights to make up for all the calories I ate this morning. Thanks for the dessert." Grier balances the containers as she backs out the screen door.

###

We meet in the parking lot located beyond the downtown high rise. True to her word, Grier straps weights to her wrists for our four mile walk. Early mornings, the restaurant delivery trucks double park in the street making their morning rounds. Service workers rinse out garbage cans and sweep off the sidewalks as we skirt them. The green boxes offer a plethora of smells for Mojo.

"Yesterday was fun." I pump my arms to keep up with her. "I like the different women in the club. Each has her own way of facing life. Even Daphne is a character. She wants attention. Eleanor is so strong and certain of herself. Alice is fighting her way along determined to make up for lost time. She had to live under her husband's control for so long and then be lost without him. I…"

"Morning, girls." Matt steps from behind a garbage truck parked at the curb. "Getting in your morning exercise?

107

Quinn, all that lard you put on isn't going away. It's packed on too well." He's wearing the same black leather vest and jeans, with a different shirt. The two day's growth of beard doesn't improve his appearance. He flicks a cigarette into the street. He's as vile as the sour garbage truck.

"Hello, Matthew." Grier tries to deflect his bitterness.

"Matt, leave me alone," I respond. Both Mojo and Grier have their fur up.

"You think a visit from Mr. Policeman, Grier's husband, is going to scare me off? Grier, you are hot today, if I do say so." He blows a long wolf whistle looking at her in her sport's bra and short shorts. "You look good in your old age." He leans back and jiggles his eyebrows. "Look here, Quinn, the bank is on the next block over, we can go to the ATM and you can make a withdrawal for me." When he grabs my arm, both the dog and my cousin take action.

Grier tries to pull me away with her free hand. As I try to yank my arm away from Matt's fierce grip, he twists it like he used to when he wanted me to cry. Fortunately, he loses his hold when Mojo jumps, clamping onto Matt's rear end. The dog's mouth surrounds the pocket where Matt keeps his wallet. Mojo's teeth dig though his jeans. The flesh would be ground beef by now if the wallet hadn't stopped the bite. Mojo maintains his hold growling and yanking, pawing up Matt's legs. The weight of the dog almost pulls Matt down to the ground.

Grier maintains her hold on the leash. When Matt raises his hands and quits struggling, she calls the dog off. "Mojo, here." She holds the growling dog by his collar. "If I were you buster, I'd move along. We don't like you."

Matt checks his back pocket as he backs away. "We're not done here." He points at me. "Missy, you haven't seen the last of me." He rubs his hip as he crosses the street. We watch him climb into his car and screech away from the curb. The only way he leaves my presence these days is with a slammed door and burnt rubber.

Begin Again, Quinn

"Are you alright?" Grier is rubbing Mojo's head, trying to settle the animal.

My arm burns from Matt's grip. "Yeah. Grier, I'm so sorry you had to be here for that. He never -" I stop. I almost reverted to covering up his actions. "The police station is on our way. Let's go. I'm tired of putting up with this."

Several men from restaurants and the parked trucks now come over to offer assistance. I wave them off. "I'm fine. We're going to the police station. Thanks for asking," I say.

We walk past Danny's store, but it's too early for him to be there. His flower boxes spray summer blooms along the front of his shop. The line of colorful sports fishing boats backed up to the walkway lifts my spirits. "Don't worry. I'm not going to let him mess up my life again," I say. I reach around her shoulder and give her a hug.

"I can't believe it happened so fast. He was rough in high school. He got worse as he aged." She shakes her head. "I don't know how you put up with him for so long."

"I put up with him because he was always around. I thought if I didn't marry him, I'd never get married. Every girl wanted marriage back then. We grew up with 'Father Knows Best' and 'I Love Lucy.'"

The moment of terror catches up with us. I sit down on a bench and lean forward. Breathing slowly I wait until my heart slows. "All right, I admit it. He still upsets me."

Grier is rubbing my back. "Come on, Sugar. We have business up the street." She starts to giggle. "Think about the bruise he'll have on his butt in the morning!" Her levity breaks the hold of our confrontation. I join her laughing. "His legs are going to look like train tracks, too. Talk about a pain in the butt!"

THIRTEEN

Friday evening I lock my front door and join the others in Tricia's car. As we hit the edge of town, Tricia picks up the conversation, revisiting our high school days, much to Eleanor's dismay. "Do you remember the history teacher we had our sophomore year? He'd peer over his glasses and try to stare me down every time I was late to class." Tricia was the gum chewing, bubble hair, "Grease" cast member look-a-like.

"Yes. He did the same thing with everyone. Remember the time his coat caught fire?" I turn to Grier and Eleanor.

Grier breaks in, "I remember."

"Girls, can we drop the remember-when's, please. I've something to discuss." Eleanor shrugs in her seat.

Tricia winks at us in the back, through her rear view mirror.

Eleanor continues. "I hope we can come up with a solution to my problem tonight. I want to visit my sister in Arizona for a month or more. Someone has to keep the investment records while I'm gone. Birdie used to help me. Quinn, Grier mentioned you kept books at one time."

"Oh, Eleanor, I kept a ledger for the co-op building where I worked. You do all this on the computer. You'll be gone a little while, can't it wait?" I shrink down in my seat behind Eleanor and eye Grier, holding my palms up and shaking my head, 'No!'

"Oh, I'm certain you underestimate your abilities." Eleanor turns around in her seat to catch my hand in her iron grip. "I'll spend a couple of mornings with you. Make some notes. It's not complicated. Really, you can't hurt the program. I'll show you how to back up everything."

Begin Again, Quinn

"I bought a computer recently. Can we load your program on mine?"

"Yes, we paid extra for the program so it could be used by more than one computer. I don't know how you survived for so long without a computer."

I survived because I didn't have the money to buy one, but she wouldn't understand.

She turns back around, letting my hand go. "I use the Internet for all my clothes shopping, correspondence and banking."

Tricia shrugs, "I have to agree. I'm lost without my computer, cell phone, pager, Palm Pilot, e-mail and Internet connections. I went whole hog." She adjusts the gold necklaces around her neck. Her bracelets jangle at the flick of her wrist. "Quinn, you were smart in school. I remember trying to copy your paper during tests."

"For heavens sake, I've heard enough about your school days. Spare me." Eleanor simmers as we drive through Havelock. She turns again in her seat, her eyebrows raised in expectation and smiles at me. "What do you say?"

"I'll consider it," I say.

"Thank you. Come over to my house next week. I'll introduce you to the way I do things. For goodness sakes, what would the club do if I died?"

Grier interrupts, "Eleanor, we couldn't survive without you, so don't talk like that." She turns to me. "I bet you could do it, Quinn."

"Someone has to learn my system. How about getting together next Monday morning?" Eleanor waits for my answer.

"I'll try to make it. Grier and I walk in the mornings." I glare at Cuz. "Would sometime around 10:30 work for you?" Since beginning my class, I'm interested in the program the club uses, but I didn't want to be the one responsible for the record-keeping.

We eat dinner in downtown New Bern, not far from the community theater. Tricia excuses herself when her pager beeps. She returns to the table with a puzzled expression on her face.

"Interesting. Did anyone know Birdie sold her house? You would think she'd have called me."

"Maybe she got an offer she couldn't refuse," Grier says.

"I can't imagine her selling without first discussing it with me. She sold it a couple of months before her death."

Grier raises her eyebrows in my direction.

"I'm curious. This club formed when?" The beginnings of a headache nag at me.

Eleanor provides a bit of history. "We organized the first week of February, six years ago. The weather was terrible that year. We couldn't play golf, you see. A few of us playing bridge started talking about investments and the idea of the club formed. It started with eight of us originally. Then we grew to ten members."

"Then who died first -- Carl Byrd, Kat's husband, Ken McNeill, then Margaret? I'd like to know the sequence."

Grier wrinkles her brow, "*Hmm*. That would be Ken, Alice's husband. He died first. He owned the insurance company with Lloyd Batts. Carl passed last year and Birdie just died. I can't remember how long ago Kat's husband died."

"This incident with Kat adds to the stew pot. Does anyone else think it's suspicious?" I ask.

Before anyone can answer, Tricia interrupts. "I want you to stop this, Quinn. If the police think it's suspicious, they'll find the answers." She shakes her jangling wrists calling the busboy to our table. "Besides, we don't have time tonight. We'll miss the show if we don't get a move on. We need the checks."

Begin Again, Quinn

Grier gives me a hard look while Tricia leads us out of the restaurant. I'm wearing my new purple slacks and top with the long multicolored big shirt, very confident with the clothes. My uncertainties play tag in my mind the rest of the evening.

###

That weekend I read another death notice in the local newspaper.

"Community Leader Mourned

Friends of P. Lawrence Odom gathered on Saturday to celebrate the life of the well-loved past mayor and council member. Born in Carteret County in 1917, Odom was a commercial fisherman, farmer and popular elected official. The only child of Perry and Muriel Odom, he was preceded in death by both parents. His passing occurred from an apparent fall in his residence. A friend, Benjamin Taylor, discovered the body after the holiday weekend.

Citizens Bank of Otway established a memorial fund to collect money from well-wishers to fund a college scholarship in his name. Throughout his elected career, Odom worked for better schools. Elizabeth Jones, executor of the estate, announced the bulk of Odom's assets would go into the Fund. Area graduates wishing to apply for scholarships need to contact the law firm of Jones, Jones and Whittington."

###

Across town, another clipping slides into the serial killer's growing notebook. Odom attended public gatherings to slap backs and shake hands. He was the typical 'good old boy' in the public eye. He attended all the political rallies eating fried fish, chicken and barbecue. Only good genes prevented his arteries from clogging up.

It took a while to reel him in, but the trust grew between the killer and the politician. Odom finally bought the reverse mortgage when he saw a phony actuarial table's potential income.

Odom liked to show off a gun collection he kept in the spare bedroom upstairs. Gravity did its work. Odom toppled down his fancy stairs. He never knew what hit him.

FOURTEEN

I wake up in a sweat. No matter how much I press Matt out of my life, he sneaks back, this time in a dream. I dreamed I was in my garden and every time I cut a blossom, it dropped in my hand and his face appeared. For a long time gardener, it's worse than finding a snake in your window box. The uneasiness shadows my morning T'ai Chi and walk.

"You have every right to be upset, Quinn." Grier reassures me.

"I can't let him haunt me. I don't know what I'm going to do." I wipe my face. "I don't suppose they've caught him yet. Sam would tell us, wouldn't he?"

"Hon, Sam will call when he finds out anything. I'm so sorry you have to go through all this again."

By the time I shower and get dressed, I've driven my fears to the back porch of my mind. Spending a few more hours at the Center may help.

"You doing your best today?" Curtis welcomes me.

"I am that, thank you for asking. Oh, by the way, if you see that car again, don't hesitate to call the police?"

He lifts his cap and nods, "Will do, Miss Quinn."

The cooking division of Help & Hands caters weddings and parties. The aroma of a clove-baked ham and a sizzling beef roast reaches me as I walk down the hall. When this much food is cooking, I know there's a wedding on the books.

As I pass the kitchen door, I remember my wedding. It was small, with a reception at the church. I know from experience, the wedding isn't as important as the marriage. I shake my head, emptying out marriage thoughts.

My students refinished a set of lawn furniture the previous week. Tomorrow leans against the wall, looking disinterested. Her newly painted red stool sits close to her bare feet. If she gets an upholstery staple in her foot, she was warned. She watches as I run my hand along the arm of the bench.

"Feel this. It needs to be smoother," I say to several class members.

A couple of the women walk over to run their fingers along the same spot. I pick up a slip of fine sandpaper and make a few runs along the grain.

"People pay us to do this right. Let's give them their money's worth." They agree, select their own pieces of sandpaper and begin gently to re-sand the wood. Some of our work is contract work, but nothing leaves my shop I don't sign off on first.

I walk back to my cubicle, grab my smock and stash my purse. Tomorrow creeps over to her stool and rubs the surface. I return, reach to feel the top of her stool and say, "How's it going?"

"What, it's not good 'nough for you?" Tomorrow crosses her arms and glares.

I go back to the bench. "Rub your hand here."

She drags herself over and leans down, as if I asked her to plunge her hand into boiling water.

Taking fine sandpaper, I buff the surface. "Now this."

Her hand moves along the surface of the furniture arm.

"Wouldn't you rather have it smoother?" Wrong question. I reword it. "Can you tell the difference?"

The girl bends, runs her hand along the wood. She pushes out her bottom lip as her fingers rub through the sanded place. She stoops to feel the wood of her own stool. "Do I have to sand all of it? I thought I was through with this ol' thing. I painted it red, like some kid might like." In spite of her words, she takes a piece of the fine sand paper from the stack on the cabinet.

Karen Dodd

There's a new pile of discarded furniture at the double door entrance to the room. I rummage through it to find something for a new class project. They need to experience repairs requiring a delicate hand. We focus on the old steamer trunk I pulled from the pile. There are labels stuck to the lid. Tarnished brass bands and wooden reinforcements run the length of each side. Dented brass shoulders grip the corners. We unfasten all the screws and bolts to pull the thing apart. The lining disintegrates in my hands, disclosing several broken ribs in the lid. Lint and dust motes fill the air. One woman draws and numbers the parts as we work. When we finish, the trunk looks like a skeleton sprawled on the floor. We break for lunch.

I want to ask Tricia some questions, but she's not working at the Center today. I call her office from the hall phone. Her partner, Gary, tells me she's out. I ask him a few questions about real estate sales. He's brusque. I learn nothing about reverse mortgages or re-sales in the area. When I return to my classroom, Marguerite approaches.

"Can I have a word?" Marguerite leads me to the storeroom and points to my purse on the floor. "Check your bag and tell me how much money is missing."

I pull out my wallet and count the bills. "I stopped at the bank before coming. This envelope had a hundred dollars in it. I'm short twenty."

"I have the culprit."

I follow Marguerite to her cramped office where Tomorrow stands scowling.

"I ain't got it. I didn't do nothing wrong." She spews out the words.

"How do you know anything's missing? I may only want to talk to you. Quinn, would you mind shutting the door, please." The administrator leans against her desk and folds her arms across her rose-colored smock. "Money is missing. Tomorrow, I saw you take something from Miss Quinn's purse. Give it to me now and apologize to Miss Quinn."

Begin Again, Quinn

Tomorrow's cold defiance chills the room.

"If I have to strip you down to find that money, I will. Now what's it going to be?"

We stare at the silent girl. Her long hair sprays about her head in tight curls. Her jaw works back and forth and her nostrils flare as she faces us.

Marguerite orders, "Take off you shirt and shorts." Tomorrow obeys, pulling off her clothes. The girl shrinks as Marguerite reaches towards her. She throws her clothes at Marguerite, who catches them like a baseball player swooping up a foul ball.

Tomorrow's insolence seeps from her pores. Even though I want to leave, my feet seem glued to the floor. I look down and around the office trying to find something to focus on besides the teenager. "Is this necessary, Marguerite?"

"Yes, I'm afraid so. She has to learn right from wrong." Marguerite searches the pockets. "Come here, child." Tomorrow stands in front of Marguerite as she searches for my missing money. The director gently pulls the bra and underpants away from the girl's body. A smug face replaces Tomorrow's glare. Marguerite pushes the clothes back. "Take off your shoes." Marguerite points to the floor. "I wasn't born yesterday."

One foot kicks off a scuffed shoe. When she kicks off the second, a folded twenty-dollar bill falls aside.

"Miss Quinn needs an apology and repayment from you, Tomorrow." Marguerite bends over to retrieve the bill and flattens it in her hand. "Quinn, when you come next week, I want you to bring in something Tomorrow will repair for you. She'll do it under your supervision, of course."

"What I got to do that for?" The girl erupts with a string of expletives.

"No talking back," Marguerite silences her. "Now, Tomorrow, I believe you have something to tell Miss Quinn."

###

I promised Eleanor one last session learning the investment club's bookkeeping. When I leave the Help & Hands Center, I drive over the bridge for my last visit before she leaves. Eleanor opens the door to her ocean front home while talking on the telephone.

"No thank you, I'm not interested in anything further. I wanted to know your current rates and potential income schedules." She listens a moment more and adamantly says, "No, I said I'm not interested." She clicks off and turns to welcome me.

"Come in, come in." She leads me back to her office. "I'm researching insurance buy–outs and reverse mortgages. Here are five pages of links and a stack of printouts on the subject."

I flip through them shaking my head. "I'm just beginning to understand all this."

"I do need a vacation." She rubs her forehead and then dismisses the thought. "I've studied actuarial tables until my eyes ache." Her papers slap down on her leg and she smiles.

"But, that's not the reason you're here." She pulls out her desk chair and offers me a seat. Pulling up another chair for herself, she reaches over to change computer screens.

I shift keys, scrolling through the program. "I'm glad the ledger sheet and the computer do all the work." I spend a few minutes going over the things she taught me the previous week.

"No one in the club dared to take on the responsibility until now. I appreciate this." She weaves her fingers together on her knee and leans forward watching me.

"It's not as hard as I thought. May I try entering something? It won't mess up anything, will it?"

"No, go ahead. You can't hurt it. Save the old records first."

"Let me add a fake stock purchase." I tab across the ledger and enter the first company that pops in my mind.

Eleanor watches. "Is KBM a company you're familiar with?

"No, Kat mentioned it to me the day I met her in the library."

"KBM isn't a public stock. That's why the price didn't fill in automatically." She pulls the pile of records back into her lap and flips through several pages.

I eye the screen. "It was some kind of insurance company if I remember right. The name stuck." After a few minutes, I admit, "I was a bit scared when I said I'd do this. I'm sure there's someone else who can help you with this if you don't like the way I do it."

Eleanor leans back in her chair crossing her legs. Her sharply creased jeans and painted toenails are the only indication of a relaxed lifestyle. "You're doing fine."

"Thanks. Did you buy the stock or whatever this KBM Company sells?" I continue to scan the screen.

"Well no, I'm still considering doing something about it. The stream of income is extremely high for the initial investment, the investment being the buyer's home. My calculations are here if you'd like to look. I thought about calling the insurance commissioner to see if they had any complaints."

She taps the files then continues, "Oh, before I forget, here's where I keep printouts of past information on the club's stock portfolio. If you need them at your house, take them." She pulls more folders from the drawer and fingers through, showing me her filing system. "I backup everything."

I turn the sheet in my note pad and write out more details. As I erase my entries, the Pac-man curser gobbles all my numbers from the dummy stock purchase. "*Whew*, I cancelled out that entry. Is there anything else I need to do?"

"I've left you a list of everything I do before each meeting. This yellow page has all your information."

"I'm sorry. I can't absorb any more today. My noggin has its limits." I stand and stretch my back, slowly twisting from side to side. "You'll be leaving Friday week and return when?"

"I bought an open-ended ticket since I haven't decided how long I'll be gone."

"Do you need a ride to the airport?"

"No, I've already arranged for a ride."

Eleanor turns. "Coffee?" I follow her out to her kitchen. She reaches into her pantry for a sack of coffee beans. "I buy the beans at the Village Grocery. I love their blended coffee."

"I buy my coffee there, too." The fragrance of the beans creates a Pavlovian reaction. My mouth waters. "Is this the Colombian blend?"

She nods above the sound of the whirring grinder then measures the amount into the filter.

I slide behind the table in her breakfast nook to admire the view. "What a panorama. You must never tire of looking out."

Eleanor brings the sugar bowl to the table and watches the ocean. "This is my favorite spot. I don't know if you do this, but I can sit here for hours."

A cloudless sky tucks behind the ocean. Six miles away I catch the Cape Lookout light winking.

"I do the same thing. I either sit in my back room or out in the yard. There's something very satisfying about watching the water. It's a refreshing indulgence after months working on the house. It's interesting we share the same simple pleasure."

Begin Again, Quinn

"I moved here after my divorce. I never tire of it. However, the surf pounds so loud when there's a strong southwester." She laughs. "Some evenings I want to turn down the volume of the crashing waves. But -- it puts me to sleep at night."

She returns to the kitchen counter to fill the creamer. "I have a great view and don't forget my morning swim." The refrigerator door has a neatly arranged display of children in various stages of growth and grins. She points to it. "The grandchildren like visiting. Since it's gotten so hot, I'm swimming in the evening, too. It eases my arthritis."

Absentmindedly she rubs her shoulders. "Getting old isn't for sissies, as they say." She turns as the coffee maker gasps its final breath. "The way these units are built they crouch down behind the dunes which keep us safe during storms. *Ha*, now watch and see the next hurricane wipe me out to sea." She pours two large mugs and brings them to the table. "Do you and Grier walk every morning?"

"Yes, even after church on Sundays. I'm trying to lose thirty pounds." I drum the table with my fingers. "I admire the way you handle things. My marriage, well the whole relationship, was a mistake. After my divorce, I shriveled up."

"We have three choices after husbands are gone." She looks out her window and stares at the horizon. "We remain an ex-wife or widow, learn to live alone or find someone else. Without the other one, we have to find who we are, first. Or so I think. Moving too fast creates mistakes."

Eleanor stares back. "I was always a survivor. I fought for my husband, my marriage and even the kids. I read a lot, set priorities, dismissed the nit-picky details of life."

"Like what?"

"Like caring what people say, pettiness, or just plain worrying about things you can't control. I don't allow worry time."

I like her attitude. "I wish I had your wisdom forty years ago. I was more like an empty shell, tossed by waves, or baking in the sun, I lost what was *me*."

"That's a good analogy, an empty shell. You're good with words, Quinn. I can tell you're a caring person. Your silence at the meetings has not gone unnoticed." She taps the table top with her thumb. "I'm glad you decided to join us."

She smiles, "I also got a very nice settlement and later, an inheritance from my parents. I was one of the lucky ones." She leans as she crosses her legs. "I've been comfortable. He's still practicing medicine. He has to. He started another family while our children were in high school."

I take another sip of coffee, "The money I inherited from my Aunt Grace was a blessing. I feel like the lilies of the field these days. "I thought I'd be working until they carried me away." Patting the table with my palms, I turn and say, "Enough about me. Tell me about your sister."

"Joanne was the carefree sister. You know what I mean?"

I nod. "Grier had a brief period of flightiness. She trashed all her blithe notions when she graduated and decided to be a teacher. She went to East Carolina College."

Eleanor looks amused to find out about Grier's errant stage. "Joanne was a fairy child flitting around, until the asthma hit. That was before the inhalers we have now. It got better as she grew older but she still had bouts in college. One doctor suggested a dryer climate. When she graduated from nursing school, she took a job in Arizona. She married Drew, but after a few years of working, she stayed home to raise their children. When the kids grew up, she became a visiting nurse. Arizona became a retirement community and eventually she moved into hospice work. Here," she hands me a black and white photographic collage. "Drew, her husband, took these shots years ago. They used to come a lot when the children were small. We were all on the beach that day."

Begin Again, Quinn

The framed snapshots look professional. I admire the sharpness and captured expressions. The sisters have identical hair coloring, noses and smiles. Glimpses of their faces reflect in their children.

"When he retired, he was going to spend more time with his photography. They built another room on the back of their kitchen and both were looking forward to his retirement." She points to the sandy haired man in one picture. "Drew died six months later, a heart problem. Joanne was lost, but she's pulled herself together now with her own grandchildren and family. Either she comes here each year or I go there. She still works part-time with hospice."

"That had to be hard for her."

"My sister and I grew even closer after he passed." She continues. "We seem in tune with one another. One of us can be thinking about the other and the phone rings and sure enough it's Sister on the line." She chuckles. "I asked her to move here, but she won't budge. She's as stubborn as I am."

"I don't know what I would have done without Grier these past few months. We're like sisters."

We chat through the hour. When Eleanor checks her watch a second time, I figure it's time to leave.

"Well, thanks for the coffee and encouragement on the computer. If you don't mind, I may come over after you're gone. I'd like to copy the data disk for my computer." I place the framed photographs back on a nearby shelf.

"Here, let me give you a key." She opens an organized drawer and pulls one from its slot.

She says, "I'll make a flash drive up for you. You do have an empty USB hookup on your computer?"

"Yes. We talked about them this week in class. I'll be interested in how it works."

"Just open it up and save to your files, then back it up when you're through. You'll do fine." She shows me what hers look like. "I'll leave it and all the files for you here on the kitchen table. I'm leaving my email address if you have questions." She carries our cups to the sink, runs water, rinses them out and immediately places them into the dishwasher.

I gather my purse and notebook. "It's supposed to storm next week. There's a low brewing in the Atlantic. I hope you're in the sky and away before it hits."

"It's an early flight."

"Reading is nice when the weather turns bad. Grier and I exchange paperback mysteries. I think I solved the 'whodunit' I'm reading now. I want to see if I'm right so I'll finish the book."

She nods. Her mind is already elsewhere. Waving goodbye, she says, "I like figuring out puzzles too."

I pull open the door to my aging Toyota and wave. The car emits a high whine and finally catches. I might be buying another car sooner than I want to.

FIFTEEN

That evening the phone rings. I hesitate before answering it, but his number is one I know.

"Hi, Quinn, it's Danny. You got a minute? Can we talk?"

"Sure, what's up?'

"I'm off tomorrow. Do you want to go fishing? My boat's not fancy. I thought we'd drop some lines in the water and trawl out to the Cape. I'll bring the food and promise to behave myself."

I haven't seen him in two weeks and I miss his company. "Sure. What can I bring?" I ask.

"Just yourself. Nancy and I haven't been hitting it off lately. I'd like some good company." He hesitates. "There's stuff I want to talk about. You've always been a good listener."

"What time?"

He says early. I hang up and go find my canvas carryall.

The next morning, I sit on the front porch waiting. He arrives before the sky turns to blue. His headlights compete with the early morning fog puffs clinging to my front yard.

The trim fiberglass boat mounted on the new trailer is an odd combination behind his old battered truck. I climb into the cab and we pull away. Traffic is busy at the boat ramp. I hold the boat next to the dock until he jogs back after parking the truck and trailer. He hops aboard and I step up from the floating dock onto his fish box at the stern.

"How'd you do that?" He asks as I step down into the boat.

"What?" I hand him my bag and he shoves it under the console.

"You looked like a cat, flowing onto the boat. You didn't need to grab onto anything to pull yourself aboard."

"Ah, you've never seen my T'ai Chi at work." I assume a Kung Fu pose and joke with him. "It has to do with balance and motion. I don't even think about it anymore."

"I'm finding out more things about you every day, Ms. T'ai Chi Master." He loosens a line from the cleat and we drift out toward the channel. "Neat trick."

"If you do it often enough, your body becomes fluid. You flow from one position to another. You should try it." I coil his dock lines for him as he takes the helm.

"Where do they teach it?"

"I saw a notice of a class. I think it was at the health food store. Call them." I sit on the passenger side of the Captain's bench seat. His fuchsia floral shirt hangs over khaki cut-offs. The warmth of his body radiates to my side.

Danny catches me looking around. "In case you're interested, the life jackets are under the bow seat. I don't expect you'll need one." He points a toe toward the front of the boat.

"Old habits again." I laugh. "I was wondering where they were. Growing up on a boat, I look for safety gear."

As the boat moves into the waterway, we leave the shoreline with its gnats and mosquitoes. The sun rises higher, shifting from a big orange globe into a scalding yellow orb. As we pass an island across from the city port, I smear my arms and legs with sun tan lotion. Danny shakes his head when I offer him some.

Two dozen boats bob in the turning basin. Morehead City is a port for ocean going tankers. Tall orange cranes unload natural rubber, chemicals, cement, scrap metal and coal from all over the world. A container ship sits high on the water along the bulkhead. Around the corner, a phosphate transport sucks cargo aboard. The monoliths tower over us as we glide past.

Begin Again, Quinn

Danny idles the motor while we select our fishing lures and plant the poles in the holders. "I've been using these little spinners." He hands me one and I mimic him, tying mine on a line. Four lines are in the water when we turn out towards the inlet. Overhead, screaming seagulls cry out.

"Hungry?" Danny reaches into a box and pulls out a Bojangles paper sack.

While I decide between a cheddar cheese or a sausage biscuit, he pours me a mug of already sweetened and creamed coffee.

My mouth waters as I pull open the foil liner. "*Umm*, good. Hope you like sausage." I hand him a breakfast biscuit with the foil pulled down.

With our fishing lines in the water, he cuts a wide arc and cruises toward the south side of Shackelford Island. Banker ponies nibble marsh grass in the distance. Kayakers camp on the north side of the island. Their bright colored tents and boats blossom like wayward flowers on the shore. This early in the morning, with wind and tide running together, the ocean is calm. We circle and pass through Beaufort Inlet between Shackelford Island and Bogue Banks. A few fishermen wave from the Ft. Macon State Park side. Pelicans glide on fingertips along the shoreline. The large birds dive, their awkward beaks slapping the water.

"Nancy's been moping around the house. It appears her fellow dumped her. I don't know whether to be happy or sad. I never had good feelings about him. Seems to me he was only interested in her until he found out I owned half of everything. Not hard to figure him out." He takes another swallow of coffee, crumpling the foil wrap in his fist and tossing it into the empty sack.

"I'm sorry." I pat his arm.

"*Ah*," he shakes his head. "The store's sales are up. More tourists are here than any past season by our records. I've installed a new inventory system. Ordering and re-sales are easier." He turns the wheel onto an easterly course. "No hurricanes. Fishing's good. You'd think I'd be pleased as a pig in poop." He adjusts his sunglasses on his croakies. His boat steers itself. "Guess I'm bored."

He kicks off his topsiders, standing to pull up the bimini overhead for shade. "Nancy might be better off if I were to break away for a while. I'm thinking about starting a new business."

"Really, like what?"

"Oh, a full-fledged restaurant would take too much of my time. Owning a sports fishing boat has appeal but the overhead would kill me the first few years. I don't want to get into sales, like boats or real estate. Thought about a different kind of store, not sure yet. You know, like expanding where we are, but with different merchandise."

"Is there space?"

"Yeah, that t-shirt and tourist trinket store isn't making it and they have three more months on their lease. The owner of the shopping strip asked me if I was interested. Nothing much has made it there in the past ten years. What do you think?"

"I have no idea. I thought every kind of place was already here." I suggest, "Grier says Myrtle Beach is way ahead of us as far as growth. Why don't you take off and go visit. Find out what's hot and what's not. I guess this area's interest will follow suit in a few years."

"Yeah, but I don't want a fad thing. Whatever I do I want it to last."

"Good thinking…"

Something hits one line and then another pole spins and bends. Soon all four rods bow under the weight of thrashing fish. For the next half hour, each time we send the lines back, another fish strikes. There's eight good-sized blues in the fish box by the time things slow down. My hands and a leg are messy with fish slime and blood splatter.

Begin Again, Quinn

"It seems like every time I get around you and fish, I get slimed." I laugh with him. The sun is beginning to bake my arms and face. I wash up with several towelettes, put on my long-sleeved shirt and apply another layer of suntan lotion. "I'm not complaining. Wow, that's the way I like to fish."

He laughs. "I guess you brought me luck today." He grins back as he wipes off his own hands. He dips a mop over the side and squeezes it.

"Now that the excitement's over, you were telling me what kind of business you wanted to open."

"Oh, I don't know, maybe an upper end art gallery or expand the coffee shop into a breakfast deli or luncheonette, maybe ice-cream. There's no small place on the waterfront for breakfast or a light lunch. I'll need to study it. Just talking out loud helps." He wipes down the deck with the mop and rinses it over the side.

His faded ball cap doesn't shade his ears, which now match his peeling sunburned nose. I peer up from under my wide brim hat as he smiles at me and shakes his head. I'll agree with Grier. He is a hunky, silver-haired man. I'm not blind to his assets. But it would be like dating my brother. I wish he would find someone else to attract his romantic interests.

"Maybe I'm getting an itch. I like the idea about Virginia Beach and maybe Myrtle Beach. There's also Beaufort and Georgetown in South Carolina, or even Charleston. I might take the big boat down the waterway and spend some time there. I can sleep on board and shower at marinas. Just piddle here and there in waterfront towns."

"I've read old *Southern Living* magazines. The towns sounded very Old South and idyllic. Maybe some day I'll journey down there." I sit back on the bench and prop a foot on the edge of the boat.

"Sure you don't want to go with me?"

I smile and shake my head. "Right now I have too much on my plate."

"Can't say I didn't try." He wipes his chin with the palm of his hand. "Okay, back to being friends again. I may take off and visit those places. I also like having you as my fishing partner like when we were kids. I haven't ruined my chances, have I?"

"Not as a fishing partner, Danny. I like fishing and I like you. Any time you want to go fishing, give me a call. I know you'd like to hear interest in another way, but it's the best I can offer."

We circle through the Cape Lookout hook, try our luck on the ocean side then return to drop anchor for an early lunch. Bottom fishing, we pick up a flounder, croakers and a few pinfish. We head back to the ramp by mid-afternoon scooting in before the big sports fishing boats roar in from the Gulf Stream. My face feels like I've baked in the oven. I help him load the boat back onto the trailer and he drives me home. While he cleans the fish at my kitchen sink, I filet and sort them into different plastic bags for freezing, leaving one nice croaker out for supper.

"What did we do before zip-locks?" He holds his bags up by the edge and shakes it. The thick fleshy fish flattens against the bottom.

"There used to be something called wax paper." I grin and walk him to the front door.

The shower prickles my sunburn, forming tiny blisters on my wrists. Fresh seafood lines my freezer. Danny and I mended our friendship. It wasn't a bad day. I pull broccoli and carrots out to steam and slice potatoes, onions and herbs over the lightly breaded fish before sliding it into the oven.

###

Wednesday morning, I'm dreading the work with Tomorrow. I walk through the house eyeing various pieces of

furniture and decide on Grace's bench. She used to have it
near her side door. Coats and magazines held down one end
most of the time or I'd find her purse, keys and mail. She'd sit
on it to take off or put on her shoes depending on whether she
was coming or going. I'd sit with her, learning to tie my shoes
or buckle my sandals. The paint's thinner in places. A few
nicks scar the arms where the heavy door banged.

As I walk through the house and remember the things
I took from her house, I feel enveloped in her arms. Grace had
a gardenia smell about her when she wasn't in the kitchen
baking. Her glasses, if they weren't perched on her nose hung
around her neck on a dark cord. She developed a carry-
across-the-playground voice during her teaching years. But
her one-on-one voice she shared with me was musical. She'd
sit on the porch swing when I was little and read to me. She
offered to pay my way to college. I wanted to get married. She
was a patient woman. Her hand-quilted patchwork today
cloaks my beds. I wish I had listened to her more.

I keep the bench in my Carolina room beneath the
windows. I manage to drag it out to the car and tie it in my
trunk. When I arrive at the Center, Curtis helps me unload
and bring it into the workshop. I put newspapers down.
Tomorrow shuffles over and waits for instructions. Together
we lift the bench onto a work table.

"There, this is a good height to work. We'll strip the
paint off down to the wood. Let's start with the legs and
braces." I point out the parts that will be more tedious to
clean as Tomorrow watches. I pile clean rags, sponges and
brushes by a stack of newspapers.

"Put these gloves on. You can't work with this stuff
without gloves." I pry off the lid of the paint remover. "Here's
a brush or you may want to try this sponge. It depends on
where you work." I dab a few strokes on one side and watch
as she follows, stroke for stroke.

"It don't seem like it's working, much." Brassy as a
bar room spittoon, Tomorrow holds her chin out as if *I* owe
her a few days work. "Do I do the whole thing like this?" She

continues to dip and coat the wood. A few drops spot the paper beneath.

"No, let's just do one part at a time. That way, we can time it to see how long to wait." I coat one end of the support dowels and watch the chemical fizz. "See how it lifts away the old finish? They're probably layers of furniture polish and wax in there. Don't get too close, Hon."

She jerks back and watches me a while before she begins again. She's careful in the corners and easily applies a smooth coat without dripping any more on the newspaper. She experiments with a sponge between the spindle rods.

"We'll wait awhile and see what it does before we do another patch." I bite my bottom lip hoping something good comes out of working together.

Her face betrays nothing. She shelved all her feelings before she came. When she finishes her end of the dowels, she looks up, almost bored. She brushes her wild mane back from her face with the back of her gloved hand.

"While it soaks, let's cut out the cushions and covers. Bring that stack of pillows when you come." I take off my gloves and she does the same. My sack of new fabric is in my cubby beside my purse.

"I'll use the old cushion as a pattern." We walk down to the sewing area of the gym and lay the old cushions on the work table. "Pull the covers off the foam and we'll cut new ones first." She watches while I slice out the new shapes from a mat of dense foam. "Take these shears and cut along the crease of the cushion covers, where the seam is."

I lay the old fabric on top of the new material. "We take these and lay it out on the new cloth and pin it down. Leave a good couple of inches between them. We have plenty of cloth."

She smoothes the bright paisley fabric across the table. "The color is better on this." She acts like a cloth salesgirl. "That old stuff was ugly as sh-." She smirks and thankfully doesn't say what she thinks.

While I walk over and check the progress of other projects going on in the class, she pins each piece by the corners of the patterns. When I return I say, "I like to use a rule to make straight lines out from the edge, like this. A good inch all around gives us a seam width. We'll trim after we sew them up." I hand her the marking chalk and yard stick and walk away again.

Her small fingers seem childlike inside the big shear's handles. Her tongue peeks out between her lips as she concentrates, cutting on the seam line. By the time she's finished cutting, her entire bottom lip disappears inside her mouth as she bites down in concentration. For a while, she forgets she's a prisoner. Checking my watch, I walk to the other end of the old gymnasium. The girl follows dragging her feet.

She toes her ankle with a dirty shoe and assumes her former self. "I don't know why I have to do this stupid work. Telling me what to do and making me fetch for you." Although her voice is low, the vehemence carries across the room to the others, who now avert their eyes from our project.

We wipe the fizzing mixture from the wood and apply another coat further up on the legs and arms. We alternate back and forth for most of the morning between the woodworking and the sewing. She sulks as I talk aloud, more for myself, showing her how to cut the fabric and sew on the commercial machine. I show her how to make a bias tape for cording.

Breaking for lunch, Marguerite walks over to inspect our progress. "Well, how's it going? Is Tomorrow doing her share?"

"She's a good helper when she puts her mind to it."

We stand admiring our progress. Tomorrow looks as if she's sucking on lemons around Marguerite.

"How is your house? You haven't mentioned any of your projects lately," Marguerite asks. "Tomorrow, Miss Quinn bought an old house and did most of the work on it fixing it up. Isn't that something for a woman to know how to do?"

The girl gives me a stony stare.

"I have to leave early today. I'm almost finished with my computer class at the community college. I think Tomorrow has the skill to finish." I glance over at the teenager.

She gives me a suspicious glare. "You want me to finish that bench without you being here? A kid could do it." Tomorrow rolls her eyes.

Marguerite nods her head and returns to her office. "I'll see you later, young lady."

Tomorrow watches Marguerite's retreat and then whips back around to me. "I don't know why an old lady wants to go to college. You tell me why." She ties her hair back with a scrape of cloth cut from my fabric, then pulls her sludge-smeared gloves back on her hands.

"I go to school to learn what I need to know. I'm finding computers are something I enjoy. Don't you like learning new things?"

Tomorrow considers my question. "I know all I got to know to live. Don't need calculus or foreign language. Why they teach us that stuff? Going to school just gets in the way of my living." She dabs her brush back in the can. "I don't want to talk no more so don't be asking me nothing." She ignores everyone as she continues her work. Using a putty knife and rags, Tomorrow gently rubs the legs clean after waiting patiently between applications.

I change my clothes and return to take a final survey at the various projects underway in the classroom. "It looks like there's nice wood under this old finish. I don't want to paint it or stain it again. I think we can use wax and polish it."

I explain what I want done by next week. "Be sure you tap the lids back in place. I don't want it to dry up and please, wipe the table off."

"Yeah, yeah, I hear you."

"When you finish taking off this finish, don't forget to re-glue the joints. You've done that before." I stop and touch her shoulders. "You did very well, Tomorrow. Thank you."

She freezes under my hand. Her rigid body slouches as I move away. "*Humph*, I'm taking a break." She slinks off to flop on one of the old couches by the wall.

At the community college, I sit at a desk with another student. Her papers have Melissa Garner on the top, but she introduced herself as Lissa on the first day of class. Her knees show through torn jeans. She layers her tank tops over her slender body. In spite of her attempt, she can't pull off the scruffy demeanor. Her nails, trimmed neatly and polished with a pale color, are as clean as her hair. She holds her head up and looks into my eyes when we talk.

"Lissa," I get her attention, "I know there are a lot of Garners in the area, but you remind me of someone I know. Are you related to Pam Garner?"

She smiles, "I can't escape my looks. Yes, she's my mother." Now that she is facing me, I notice other similarities in her eyes and mouth.

"She and I are in the same investment club."

"Are you? I've only met one person from that group." One eyebrow goes up. "I don't know why mother hangs out with her." Her mouth does a little quirky thing.

"*Ah*, I understand. My Daddy always said if you can't say something good about a person, don't say anything at all." I pat her shoulder, "Give your mom the benefit of the doubt. I need to pay more attention to her, myself. I'm new and I haven't gotten a chance to get to know her."

"Ever since Daddy left, she's changed. She doesn't go clothes shopping with me. I don't think she's gone to a movie in a year. I wish she'd go out more and make new friends." She swings her hair off her shoulder. "Daddy and Mr. George are law partners."

"I see. I guess your Mom and Daphne George have been friends a while." Another image of mystery-solving Jessica Fletcher flits by.

"I don't know if they are friends. They were wives of business associates. Mrs. George is like the queen bee ever since they met." Lissa makes a fist and bounces it off her knee. "I wish she'd, oh, I don't know. I wish she'd be her old self."

"Well, it took me a long time to get over my own marriage. She might be interested in coming to some of the classes at Help & Hands. I'm embarrassed to say it took me over thirty years to get group counseling. Several separated and divorced women take classes and group counseling there. It may give her a chance to talk through her feelings. You could come too if you'd like."

"I don't know if she'd go. Maybe if I say I need her to go with me…"

"That's a generous offer. I wish you luck." I pack up my books and notes.

She does the same. "Where is this place?"

I tear a sheet out of my notebook and write down the information. "While you're there, come down the hall and visit my class. I teach furniture refinishing and upholstery."

"Cool and you're a computer wizard, too." She taps my computer console then waves good bye. "I've enjoyed our talk." As she walks away, I see the mother's walk in the daughter.

I'm delighted the following week, when I arrive, my bench is ready to take home. I run my hand over the arms and

136

legs. The waxed and buffed wood feels like marble. She studies me from her corner perch. "Tomorrow, this is wonderful. You must have worked on it every day since I saw you last."

Her eyes betray her satisfaction but her mouth doesn't twitch as she walks over. "So, you satisfied? That ol' woman, in that office, she worked me like a slave driver. She wouldn't let me go until I did my best. 'Do your best,' all she kept saying."

Trying to dissolve her rancid remarks, I say, "I don't think I could have done better." I examine the bias cording and zipper on the cushions. "Who helped you finish these? They're perfect."

"That woman over there showed me how." She points to the Vietnamese woman in my class. "It wasn't hard to do. I finished the second one all by myself."

"Well, you certainly did a marvelous job. I'm proud of you."

"*Humph*," this time her stance is not as defensive. Her hands rest on her waist.

"Didn't she do a beautiful job?" The Center's director comes toward us with a satisfied smile on her face. "All I did was watch. She knew what she was doing." She tries to pat Tomorrow's shoulder but the girl draws away. "She still has an attitude but now I know she can do good work. It's all about doing her best."

"Marguerite, would it be all right if Tomorrow helped me load this in my car and take it home? I'd like her to see where it's going. She can help me unload the bench so I don't scratch it."

"You sure?" Marguerite waits for me to nod and then she turns to the girl. "Miss Quinn asked if you can go with her to help her take this bench home. Do you mind?"

Tomorrow glares at the director. "Sure, sure. Whatever it takes to get me away from you and this stinky ol' place. This smell is beginning to bother me." She squinches up her face and waves a hand by her nose. She goes over, puts on her shoes and waits for my directions.

Using discarded cushions, we line the trunk and tie the bench inside. "I'd hate to have it scratched after all your hard work."

Tomorrow runs back inside and brings out the new cushions. She throws them in the rear seat and climbs in on the passenger side. The engine does its hard crank and finally turns over.

"You sure have a trashy old car. How come you drive this piece of junk? I bet you have lots of money and you can get a new one." She fiddles with my dead radio dials as I drive.

"As long as this one gets me where I want to go, I'll keep it. A dear friend left it to me when she died. It's more than metal, foam and wheels to me."

"*Uh-huh*," Tomorrow rolls her eyes into the top of her head.

"It has a sentimental value. Haven't you ever had something you treasured or didn't want to let go?"

"Never had anything to -" she snarls, "treasure."

"Do you have your driver's license?"

"Sure, my granny lets me drive her. She's so pokey. She sits crouched over and peeks through the wheel." The girl almost laughs describing the woman. "She's old and she don't understand about things. She go to work and she come home. She gets her check and she buys groceries. I get an allowance from her." Tomorrow pats the short denim skirt and knit top. "I got my own money to buy stuff. I don't need her handouts."

When we arrive, she studies my house from the driveway. "This where you live?" I unlock the door and prop the screen open before we go back to the car. We untie the trunk lid and lift the bench out, sitting it on the ground.

Begin Again, Quinn

"Wait, I'll get the new cushions." Tomorrow pulls open the car door and grabs them. She carefully sets the cushions in their place. "It does look pretty, doesn't it?" It's the first time I've heard any satisfaction from her.

"You did a professional job, Tomorrow. You could probably find work with an upholsterer if you were interested in pursuing it when you get out of school. I'd recommend you go to the community college and get some business basics. One day you could open up your own shop...."

"There you go again. Talking school, work, *duh*, the old white woman's dream for me. You haven't a clue, do you?"

I bite my lip and shift my weight to lift my end of the bench. She does likewise and we carry the bench into the house, down the hallway and into the back room. As we pass through the hall, Tomorrow peers into each room.

"It goes here under the window." We center it along the wall. "It's a good match, don't you think?"

She pouts her chin out and nods her head. "*Uh-huh*. My granny grows flowers like those." Her all seeing eyes have taken in my house and yard in minutes. "When I was little I'd cut some and put them in a can on her breakfast table. Hers are bigger than yours."

"Those are zinnias, one of my favorites. Would you like some tea or a glass of water before I take you back?" She follows me into the kitchen.

"You painted this house yourself?" She runs her hands along the counter tops and fingers the sink fixtures.

"I refinished the wood floors, painted it all, laid this tile in the kitchen and bathrooms and even hung the ceiling fans." I point to the fan as I pour our glasses of tea.

She glances up and watches the spinning fan for a moment.

"A woman can do anything she wants if she sets her mind to it," I remind her.

Karen Dodd

She sips the tea as I talk. "Yeah, yeah, yeah. There you go preaching at me again. Do you preach to everyone?" She stands up from the counter stool. "My granny goes to a preacher lady. You should have been a preacher lady instead of a teacher at that crummy place for beat up women."

I remain sitting. "Would it surprise you to know I was once one of those beat up women?"

Tomorrow walks toward the door and stops. "Yeah?" She turns back to me. "Is he in jail or did you kill him?"

"Neither. It was a long time ago and I got away from him. Would I be preaching at you again if I told you, you can change your life?"

"Sure, right, lady. Why do you think I want to change my life? I may like it the way it is. I got no am-bition" she draws out the word, "to *be* anything different. As soon as I can get out of this town, I ain't never gonna come back. So don't get any high cotton white lady's ideas about this child!" She puts her glass in the sink and wipes the counter top with her hand. "How about you take me back now?"

I lock the door and drive her back to the Help & Hands Center. Once she gets there, she resumes her slouch, finding a spot on the dilapidated couch in the corner.

Begin Again, Quinn

SIXTEEN

As I drive over to Eleanor's to pick up the materials she left, big raindrops bullet the windshield and parking lot puddles. Double-parked, I hurry up to her door -- sliding on the wet deck. The key fits snugly into the lock but doesn't turn, even after I jimmy it back and forth.

Finally, the lock gives and the door swings open. Flipping on the hall light, I notice a sweet smell. I feel like someone might step out of a door and grab me as I walk down the hall. The hairs on the back of my neck tingle.

I'm relieved to find the files and folders stacked neatly along with a flash drive on the kitchen table. A mess of papers and file folders lay on the floor and across Eleanor's desk. Her desk drawers are open and files askew. She must have forgotten something in the last minute. The wind from the storm plays tricks on my imagination when the floor creaks overhead causing another shiver to run along my spine. A loud thunder roll follows a lightning crack.

I shake my head to toss off the willies. One of Eleanor's canvas carry-all bags is looped over a door knob. I shove the pile of papers and folders inside, hug them to my chest and relock her dead bolt, my back to the pelting rain. The next bolt of lightning zigzags overhead as I reach the car. Wiping the rain from my face, I flick the windshield wipers to high while turning the defroster full blast. Sheets of rain pour off the windshield. The back of my head still tingles as the wind buffets my car over the high-rise bridge. I wrangle the car against the wind leaving thoughts of Eleanor's home on the other side of the bridge.

###

Drying off after a late night shower, I hear a distant siren. I barely have time to slip into my bathrobe before the phone rings.

Grier says, "Hey, Hon, hate to bother you, but there's a fire over at the beach. It sounds like it might be near

Eleanor's townhouse. Didn't you go over there this afternoon?"

"Yeah, just at dark. How'd you know there's a fire over there?" I yawn. "I heard the alarm here a few minutes ago."

"This is another romantic evening for us, darling. There was nothing on television. Sam decided, on his one night off, to turn on the scanner. I fell asleep on the couch. They're calling in surrounding fire stations to help. It sounds like a bad one. We may drive over to see."

"You'll be awhile." My night stand clock indicates midnight. "Call me in the morning. It's supposed to rain tomorrow, so I guess walking in the morning is out."

As a fire truck's siren passes the neighborhood I hang up. My home's original owners put up insulation, thin paneling and bare plank flooring upstairs, but left the room unfinished. My inclination is to use it as a hidey-hole and storage. I like to sit on the window seat and read, especially when it rains. I climb up without turning on the bare ceiling light to peer over to the ocean. The gusting wind blows a staccato of raindrops cooling the window glass. The beach town glows softly through the rain, but I can't see a fire. A channel marker blinks red across the waterway.

Downstairs, I make a cup of Earl Grey and carry it, with Eleanor's canvas bag, to the bedroom. I'm wide-awake after the phone call, stair climbing and fire sirens. Spreading out Eleanor's things, I sort through the stack. Among the folders are notes on KBM with all her printouts. Eleanor must have grabbed them up by mistake.

The next morning, I troll out under an umbrella to fetch the morning paper. My eyes scan my usual favorites and then I fold a page back to begin my puzzles. When the phone rings, I jump.

"It was Eleanor's! I couldn't see anything but flames last night. The smoke was awful. I bet they could see the flames all the way down to Emerald Isle," an upset Grier wails. "They kept spraying the fire wall to keep other units from burning. Fire trucks came from all over the county."

"Lord! Did anyone get hurt?" I think about the empty parking lot. "Do they know how it started -- wiring or lightning strike?"

"Nope, I can't tell you how it started. The fire was contained in her building and no one else was home."

"Well, that's a good thing. I'll have another blessing to add to my morning count."

"The weather forecast has upgraded us to a tropical storm. It'll rain all day. What you doing?"

"I did my T'ai Chi and jogged in place, read the paper and am now working on the crossword puzzle. Then I'm tackling Eleanor's program."

"So you did get everything you needed to run the program?" Her fingers tap against the receiver, as if she's sending Morse code.

"Yep, I went through the things she left me last night. I need to load the program for my first run. You don't suppose this is another unexplained accident for our club members, do you?" The nagging thought surfaced as soon as I knew it was Eleanor's home.

"Oh my gosh, I hope not. I don't even want to think about it," she says.

"Did someone call Eleanor?"

I take a bite of whole grain toast and chew on it while Grier tells me about their call to Eleanor. Grier will pick her up at the New Bern airport. As I hang up I remember the jumbled papers and files she left in the office, or did she? I'll have to mention it to Sam.

###

143

The next day, the storm front slowly moves up the coast. New waves of heat blow across the Sound. I wake up at 6:00 and can't get back to sleep. With the storm over, the electricity in the air gives me a power surge of my own. We didn't walk and I have energy to burn. Following my T'ai Chi, I fix my first cup of coffee and decide to make bread.

Vonceal was a friend I made while Matt was stationed at Ft. Bragg. Mrs. Doerr, Von's mother, visited for a week. She taught us how to make yeast bread, stickies and doughnuts. I'd written "Mrs. Doerr's Bread" on the faded recipe card. I still bake her bread.

While the yeast puffs up in warm sugar-water, I measure out the flour and other dry ingredients. Because of the moisture in the air, I use a bit more flour in the mix. Pounding the dough, I knead out my morning energy.

I leave the bread to rise and decide with the wet soil, it would be a good time to weed and work in my yard. By late morning, the bread is baked and I'm putting in a tray of annuals around the fountain.

"Told you I'd come back didn't I," Matt whispers as if he's talking to a child. His voice startles me.

I turn and stand so he has to squint in the sun to see me. Trowel in hand, I face him. "That's it, Matt. I've taking out a restraining order against you."

"Yeah, the nice policeman explained all that to me a few days ago. There's no call…"

I can look him in the eyes and no longer flinch.

"Now Quinn, don't do anything you'll regret. You don't want to see me in prison, do you? Let's try to remember the good times we shared."

"I don't remember any good times, Matthew."

"I don't scare too well, Quinn-girl. I came to get what you owe me." There's a different air about him. The aggression is gone, but the meanness remains. "All I want is a little bit of money, Quinn, to tide me over until my ship comes in. Don't go talking warrants and jail wi-"

"Is there a problem, Quinn?" Charles calls from his yard. He walks slowly around the end of the picket fence and stands by my rose trellis.

"Oh, so you got a boyfriend now, have you? First a dog attacks me," he rubs the back of his hip, "and now you're calling in the Marines?" Matt sizes up Charles with one quick glance and steps back. "Ain't that convenient?"

"I'm calling the police." I take a deep breath and wave at Charles. "No problem. He's leaving. In fact he won't ever be coming back."

"*Humph.*" Matt's legs are planted wide on the ground and his hands are tucked in his back pockets as he stares first at me and then at Charles.

I walk up to the porch and reach inside the door for the phone. I have Sam's cell number on speed dial. I like this new phone. "Yes, Sam, Matt is back." As I turn my back on Matt, I hear his swift steps move around the corner of the house. "Can you send someone out immediately?"

Charles follows Matt and then waves his hand to me. "All clear, here." He walks back to our fence and picks up his hoe where he dropped it. "Are you all right?"

"Thanks, I'm fine."

He gives me a two finger salute and returns to his morning weed patrol.

By early afternoon, I've forgotten about lunch until the phone rings. "Quinn, this is Grier. I just left Eleanor. Tricia's helping her find a place to stay and letting her use the office as a base to make all her calls."

"How is she? Eleanor doesn't seem like a woman who'd let anything get the better of her."

"Sam wants to talk with you for a bit. Would that be all right? I'm tagging along." I hear Sam mumble something. "We could be there in thirty minutes."

"Sure come on. I've been up since before the rooster crowed." Running on several cups of coffee, plus the burst of adrenaline from Matt's visit, I continue, "Have you eaten yet? I baked bread this morning. I'll have sandwiches made by the time you get here."

"Are you sure? We haven't eaten and that sounds wonderful."

"No problem," I insist. "Sam hasn't seen the house." I hang up and put away my gardening tools.

Inside I slice into a loaf of bread. I add grapes to chopped chicken, toasted pine nuts, celery and salad dressing.

Eleanor's folders spray across the table. I stack them into my milk crate filing system. A Raleigh consignment shop sold me six crates. I've yet to replace them with a real file cabinet.

Hearing a car door slam, I rush to the porch to find Charles carrying a huge gift-wrapped box. "What on earth, Charles?" I step back opening the door.

"Well, I hadn't got you a housewarming gift."

"You gave me the wind chimes," I remind him.

"Oh, that was," he hesitates, "a peace offering. I saw this at Staples this morning. It's not much. *Mmm*, something smells good."

"I baked bread."

He sees my prepared lunch. "I better go. You're expecting company."

"You'll do no such thing," I say. "By the way, thanks for being so visible this morning. I know I can handle Matt, but your presence made a difference in how fast he left."

"That's what I'm here for, anytime," he replies.

He knows how to follow orders so I tell him to sit as I reach for another glass.

Begin Again, Quinn

"I haven't opened your gift yet. You can't leave until I do that. Grier and Sam Dew are dropping by." Before he objects on being included, I reach into the icemaker and fill a glass. "Hope you don't mind unsweetened -- I cut back on sugar."

He nods.

"I still have some of my grandmother's cake." I wink at him, which surprises us both. He watches me make a fresh fruit salad of kiwi, melon and strawberries. As I finish the last plate, my other guests arrive.

Grier eyes Charles as she enters. "Charles, it's good to see you. This is Sam, my husband." She tosses her purse on the counter. "You've prepared a feast. You shouldn't have." Grier pours on her drawl for Charles' benefit.

"Yes, I should. My house is finally finished and I haven't invited you and Sam over. Charles dropped by and everything's ready. Let's eat."

Not one to chitchat or linger, I place all the plates on a tray. "Grier, would you pour the tea and bring it out to the back room?" We sit. "Let's bless it." I grab a hand each from Charles and Sam while Grier grabs hands from the other side of the table. "We used to do this when we were girls and I have so many blessings today." We all bow our heads. "Dear Heavenly Father, we thank you for the food before us, the friends beside us and the love between us. Amen."

We drop hands and I take a deep breath, smiling.

"My neighbor and best friends are eating with me. Everything's perfect." I pick up my sandwich and take a big bite. "But, why are you looking at me, Grier, Sam?"

Sam speaks first, "Charles, I'm glad you're here. It seems we have a problem. I'd feel better knowing someone is watching out for this lady for a while."

"What has Matt done now?" I ask.

"It's not him I'm worried about. At least I don't think it's him. Matt is cooling his heels in jail. I need to talk about Eleanor," Sam says. "An arsonist burned down Eleanor's condominium. I'm beginning to think it's somehow related to the membership of that investment club." To Charles he says, "Quinn recently became a member of the Golden Girls Club. I'd rather be on the side of caution with you watching out for her."

I interrupt, "It didn't mention arson in the paper. Why didn't you tell me?" I look at Grier. "What a horrible thing to happen. Oh my, I was over there." I pause, "Am I a suspect?"

"At this point, everyone in the investment club is suspect," Sam says.

"Gracious. That means us, Trish, Daphne. Sam, I don't know what to say."

"Tell me about your visit to Eleanor's house."

"It was pouring down rain when I got there."

Sam asks, "What time did you go and did you notice anything unusual?"

"It must have been around seven. It was still light, but raining cats and dogs. Her office drawers were open and files pulled out. I thought it was unusual, because Eleanor keeps everything so tidy. I grabbed things she left for me off the kitchen table and left almost as soon as I got there." I think about it a minute more. "I didn't smell anything burning, but there was a sweet odor - can't place it though."

"Was the door locked?"

"Well, I had some trouble opening it."

Grier interjects, "I don't think it was just arson. Sam, I think someone wanted to kill Eleanor just like they tried to kill Kat!"

I stop slicing a bite of melon on my plate. "What?" I think for a minute adding up all the facts. "You could be right. It's another near miss."

Begin Again, Quinn

Charles jumps in, "Do you have any proof all this is connected?"

"Normally on weekends, Eleanor volunteers at the Maritime Museum." Grier informs us, "She usually gets in late and goes to bed. Very few people knew she left town."

"I'm not supposed to give out information, but since Grier's mouth won't shut up," Sam glares at her "the arson expert says the mechanism and accelerant are found on the Internet, as well as the instructions on how to use it."

While I fix dessert, my mind fast forwards through all the information. While Grier stacks the used dishes on a big tray, I put a generous dollop of whipped cream on each slice of Granny's cake. We eat the dessert quietly. I'm thinking about all the suspects and possibilities.

Sam admits, "The timing device detonated just before midnight. If Eleanor had been home, she might have been trapped upstairs, probably asleep by then."

Swallowing that bit of information along with my tea, I shake my head.

"The entire downstairs was engulfed in flames when the first fire engine arrived. No one else lives in those end units. Luckily the weekend residents weren't down." Sam glances at his watch. "Grier, I have a few calls to make before I come home. Do you want to stay here or shall I take you home?"

Sheepishly she answers, "Sorry about blabbing it all out, but Quinn and Charles are only trying to help. They're friends, for goodness sakes!"

Sam grinds his teeth.

"Take me home. I'll walk the dog while it's still light. Don't worry. I'll double bolt the doors. Don't be late coming home, though."

She picks up the loaded tray of dishes. "We hate to eat and run, but now you know the situation. Charles, I'm so glad to see you here."

"I told Charles about Matt. He knows," I tell Grier while we are in the kitchen.

"He took it in stride. Good." Grier stacks plates with the glasses. "Lunch was marvelous. Sorry we ruined it with all this talk about murder and mayhem."

Charles stands. "No, no. You go on. I'll help Quinn with the dishes." He places the chairs back along the wall. "I'm glad to be of service. I think your imagination is taking a flying leap here. Sam will have it all straightened out soon and don't worry. I'll keep an eye out for this one." He points to me with his chin.

"See here, y'all. I've been taking care of myself for a long time." I press my lips together and squint back at them. "I won't have anyone watching out for me. I lived in Raleigh remember. I learned to lock my doors and windows. Sure, I'm upset about what happened. Matthew coming back hasn't been a joy either, but no one's obligated to look out for me." Glaring through my bifocals, I frown at all three of them. "It's the first time I'm a suspect in two attempted murders and a third successful one."

"What do you mean, a third?" Sam asks.

"Why, I'm talking about Margaret Byrd, of course. That started all this. If Danny Bridges hadn't mentioned his suspicions of a serial killer who preys on single retirees, I'd never have stuck my nose into it. Now you think I'm a suspect."

"Whoa, whoa, slow down. Now you're really stretching things out of shape. Margaret Byrd has nothing to do with this and I don't want you thinking about or doing anything, Quinn," Sam interjects. "Don't go playing detective." Sam insists.

"Right," I say.

Charles winces as he ushers them out the door. He turns and picks up his gift. "You haven't opened my present yet. You open it and then we'll clean up the dishes."

I relax a little. "You didn't need to get me anything. I'm sorry to drag you into all this."

"I'm glad to be included in your circle of friends, Quinn. After the little incident this morning, I ran into town to pick up a few things I need. I felt like this was what you needed. Now open it," he prompts.

SEVENTEEN

I drag the huge present into the Carolina room and bend on cracking knees. "I don't know why you think you can...."

"It's something I'm beginning to enjoy, neighbor." Charles smiles, watching me open the package.

Under the wrapping papers, I find a huge plastic tub and lid. "How nice..."

"Open it," Charles says.

I pull off the lid and peer inside. "Is this what I think it is?"

I feel like a child on Christmas morning. "You must be a mind reader. See, I was using old milk crates to stack things as it was," I carry the crate into the office and begin to rearrange the containers around the computer monitor and along the wall. "How thoughtful. When I saw the large Rubbermaid tub, I thought it was a strange gift. Now I understand."

"I'm glad you like it. You've repaid me in full with lunch. Can I have another piece of your cake if I stay to help you wash up?"

My earlier annoyances at Matt, finding out about the arson, becoming a suspect and then, treated like an addle-minded adult, melt. "If you want to do dishes, I can cut cake."

He rolls up his sleeves and takes off his watch. "I can do these few things by hand."

"Are you trying to distract me?" The counter cuts a ridge in my hip as I lean against it. "If you think I'll forget about the earlier aggravations -- I haven't. I only met Eleanor a couple of months ago. I feel awful for her."

Begin Again, Quinn

There's a knock on the door. I peer out the window and see a familiar truck. This could be interesting. I open the door and Danny stands there with a pile of magazines.

"Hey, Quinn. I thought maybe you could lo…" He stops in the hall when he sees Charles washing dishes. Danny sets the magazines down and offers his hand. "I'm Danny Bridges, an old friend of Quinn's."

Charles dries his hands on the dish towel draped over his shoulder. "Charles Goodwin. I'm Quinn's neighbor." He nods his head to the side. "I live next door."

I watch them. They stand, shaking hands and assessing each other. Charles, trim hair and smooth shaven face, in a relaxed military stance is carefully dressed in creased slacks and laundry pressed shirt. He faces Danny. My old friend needs a haircut and a shave. Danny looks like a beach bum in flip-flops, big pocketed rumpled shorts and toucan-print shirt.

He speaks first as he pulls back his hand from Charles's firm grip. "I'm thinking about expanding my business. Quinn offered to help me." He turns. "Do you have time to read through these?" He should have called first.

Charles crosses his arms over his chest and leans against the sink watching us.

There's a different timbre to Danny's voice. One I imagine he used in that high paying job he once held. "If you don't have time - hey, why don't I leave these with you and I'll talk with you later." His mouth forms a straight line and I detect a hurt in his eyes. "I have to go out of town for a while."

"I'll be glad to look them over. I've never seen some of these magazines." I shuffle through the stack and note colored post-it notes sticking out of the pages.

"I've marked several things I thought might work here. I wanted your opinion." Danny turns to Charles, "Nice to meet you." He pats my arm and leaves, quickly going through the door.

"Was that as awkward for you as it was for him?" Charles watches Danny back out of the driveway.

"We've been friends since grade school. He's my fishing buddy and a part of my life."

"You don't have to explain. It's obvious he's a good friend. Maybe I'm intruding on his turf." One of his eyebrows rises.

"No, we're just friends, although he wishes it were more."

"It's been a busy day for me, meeting three men in your life. Anyone else I need to know?" He teases me.

"No." I smile. "I'm involved in a few things, yes, but you are part of my life now."

"*Hmm*," he grunts and turns back to the sink to resume his washing. "Glad to hear it."

I busy myself, putting things away. "I don't know what I'll say to Eleanor." I frown. "Thinking about what Sam said, all the members of the club are suspects."

"He told you to stay out of it, Quinn."

"I'm glad Sam is finally listening. There are several things I keep stumbling over in my mind."

"I repeat. He told you to refrain. I don't want you hurt."

He finishes stacking the last plate in the dish rack and reaches for the silverware. "Several months ago, if you told me I'd be here eating a meal with you and washing your dishes, I'd have told you, you'd be sadly mistaken. Somehow, here I am." He pauses while he wipes soap from the edge of the sink. Once again, he reaches for the dishtowel on his shoulder, dries his hands and folds it over the door rack. "Now I'll take that piece of cake, if you don't mind." He turns, this time with both of his bushy eyebrows going up, like Groucho Marx.

Begin Again, Quinn

"You have a way of making me forget what I'm doing." Heat crawls up my neck as I slice another piece of cake for both of us. We walk back to the Carolina room to enjoy it. He cups a hand under his paper napkin. Once again, we sit and stare out the back windows, saying nothing. It's comfortable and I think he enjoys it, too.

"Well, I have things to do. I'll see you later. Will you be okay?" Charles tosses his napkin in the trash can under the sink and leaves.

As soon as Charles steps off my porch, I telephone my cousin. "How do I reach Eleanor?"

She's breathless. "I had to run to answer the phone. Just got in from walking Mojo."

"I'm thinking about something Sam said. I may have an idea about this."

"No, no, no. Sam said for us to stay out of it. Lady Friend, you better let him do the detecting. As for reaching Eleanor -- I suppose you could call Tricia. She would know. Now, my dear, let's change the subject. What's with the sudden interest from your neighbor? I thought things were cool between you two." She pauses. "Stop, don't start yet. I want to latch the door and get something to drink."

She puts the phone down. Her refrigerator spits ice cubes into a glass and I hear water running.

"Okay, my feet are bare and I'm sitting on our window seat, leaning back on plump cushions, girlfriend, just like when we were teenagers. Lord have mercy, if our Mamas could see us now. Okay, now, tell me all about him."

"Don't get too comfortable. There's other news. Danny dropped in while Charles was doing the dishes."

"Really? Tell me more."

"They were like two kids, sizing each other up. Interesting scene and I couldn't do anything. Danny dropped some magazines by. He wants to open another business and asked me to help him evaluate possibilities."

"Very interesting. Who left first?"

"Danny."

"*Uh-huh*, well the pecking order is established. How do you feel about that?"

"There's not a whole lot to say. I'm in no hurry one way or another."

"So, when did all this start with Charles?"

I hedge. "I guess it started when he carried in my computer or maybe it was the walk we took one evening. I know he likes Granny's orange fruitcake. He stayed and asked to wash the dishes today for another piece. While I think of it, let me bolt my door, too."

"What? Don't go away after you say that."

I check both doors before settling back on my own couch.

"You've been holding out on me, cousin. Ouch, how did I ever sit this way for long periods of time when I was a kid? My back is no longer built for this pose. Let me get up." The sounds of her groaning and rearranging come through the line. "When did you go for a walk with him?"

"Oh, it was a while back. He told me about mutual funds and annuities. I thought I told you."

"*Nooo*. We have some catching up to do on tomorrow's walk," she says and we chat for another twenty minutes.

"Yawn." I shake my head trying to knock away the tiredness. "I need to take a nap, so let me go."

"Too much action in the men's department if you ask me," Grier kids. "Bye, sweet dreams."

"Wait. Before you hang up, have you seen Katherine Knowles recently?"

Begin Again, Quinn

"I called Kat last week. She's fine and wants to know when we can play golf. I guess she's all right. She has to watch what she eats and drinks. She bought one of those medical alert bracelets."

"I thought I'd go see her. I need to call Tricia, anyway. I want to talk with them both before I tell Sam about my hunch."

"Listen. There's the doorbell. It's Julia with the grandkids. Remember to let me know what you find out and you keep me informed on that friendly neighbor."

I doze off. After waking, I reach for my address book and telephone Kat first. "Kat, are you busy tomorrow? I walk in the morning with Grier. I'd like to come by afterward?"

"Please do. I'm so antsy lying around here and taking it easy." Kat's voice bubbles over the phone.

"Around ten? Do you need anything?"

"My dear, all I need is my sanity back. I finally made it to the beauty salon this morning. I'm tired of being treated like an invalid. Lee, poor thing, called me a dozen times this week."

"At least he cares. I'll see you tomorrow." I hang up and look up Tricia's number at the office.

Tricia answers her phone and I ask, "Is there any way I can find out who sold a house -- the owners, the broker in a couple of counties around here?"

There's a long pause before Tricia says, "You go on line for some - like in Craven. You enter an address name and the history pops up, but in Carteret County, where we live, you need to go to the Register of Deeds office. You won't see the broker, but you will find the past owners and all the history on the property. Can I help you with something?"

"Yeah, if I gave you a list of names and addresses could you let me know the past three owners." I think about the growing stack of death clippings in my basket, knowing it will take a while to research them all. "Don't go back more than three years."

"What is this about?" When I tell her, Trish warns me about meddling. "You shouldn't stick your nose where it doesn't belong. You can get hurt, Quinn. Let the police handle it." I hear her shifting through papers. "I've got a busy week ahead of me. Don't know when I'll get a chance to work on it for you."

"There's no a big rush." I stand up doing a few stretching exercises. "It's been some kind of day. I'm going to heat up corn chowder for supper, then take a long bath. See you."

Before retiring for the evening, I straighten the pillows on the couch, glance around the room and turn out the light. While going down the hall I wonder if I should get some shades. It feels like someone's watching me, again. A disquieting tingle runs along the back of my head and down my spine. Matt is in jail for the night, so no need to worry about him peeking inside my house. It's probably Charles looking out his back window.

###

"Accident Claims Life

Henry R. Tucker, age 75, of Cape Carteret was killed in an automobile accident early Thursday morning. There were no witnesses. If you have any information about the accident, please call the local police department.

The car driven by Tucker flipped over the median at the intersection of Holman and Highway 24 just after midnight. It caught fire immediately. By the time rescue workers arrived at the scene, the heat of the fire was too intense to rescue the driver. Tucker's wife, Lorraine Henderson Tucker of Concord, MD, predeceased him. Tucker retired from AT&T on Long Island. He was a resident of the town for seven years. He was an avid boater and past Commodore of the Swansboro Yacht Club. Tucker was a Master Mason, member of the Scottish Rite. Tucker served as past president of City Investments and deacon in the Cape Carteret Presbyterian Church."

Begin Again, Quinn

Before heading out, I clip the new accidental death notice, as well as a basket of roses.

Kat says, "Oh, how lovely. They have such a wonderful fragrance." She motions me to follow her into her sunny kitchen.

"Sometimes the smell is bred out of them. It makes for a bigger bloom. I chose this kind specifically for its fragrance."

"I wondered why roses have no smell these days." Kat's buttercup yellow outfit radiates her zest. "Let me fix us a glass of tea. I started using the raspberry flavor like you suggested. Now, it's my favorite." Her nervous energy propels her around her kitchen. "There we are." Kat slides a tall glass over. She moves a step stool to the refrigerator. "I have a crystal vase up in this cupboard."

Kat climbs the stool to reach the cabinet. She fills the vase with water, turns off the spigot and arranges the roses.

"Nice nails. One of these days I may get mine done." We both stare at my nails.

"*Tut-tut*, you need help, bad. Gracie at Nail Illusions, bless her heart, does mine. When you want to have yours done, I'll give you her number."

"I'd like that." Self-consciously, I fold my fingers into my palms. "Do you remember when we met at the library? You were looking up KBM Company on the computer. If you don't mind me asking, what was their response?"

Kat stops, wipes her hands on a towel and thinks for a moment. "Good question. I'll talk about anything but my recent accident." Kat walks from the kitchen to another room. She returns with a large folder and pulls out a brochure and contract. "I know this appears daunting." She flips through the glossy pages. "This is what I did. They buy your old insurance policy, continue to make payments on it and when you die, they receive the death benefit.

"Right after we married, my husband and I bought two policies. These days twenty-five thousand dollars doesn't

159

begin to cover the needs of a surviving spouse. Life was so simple back then. Of course, when Tom died, I collected on his. My policy had a small cash value."

"You don't need it anymore?"

"No. I have no heirs, except my nephew. Anyway, I filled in the forms. Oh, it was one of those where the death benefit doubles if you die from an accident." She slaps the brochure shut and crosses her hands on top.

"So you did it -- you sold your insurance policy?"

"Yes, they're the owners and beneficiaries. I need to buy a new car this year. I'll use the money to boost my buying power. I thought it was a good deal. Why are you interested?" She waits while I glance though the brochure. "Curiosity killed the cat, my mother always said." She grins like the Cheshire. "Do you have some old policies?"

"No. I remember you were interested. Can I take this and bring it back later? I'd like to read through it."

"It's a done deal, so take it. I won't be around when they put in a claim." She smiles, making a joke about it.

We take our tea to her screened in porch and talk. After we part, I return home, clean house and read. When it cools, I go out and deadhead a few of my flowers. I forget to turn on the computer to get the information to Tricia or do my own research.

EIGHTEEN

When Grier honks the next morning, I scramble down my steps, stop and wave at Charles before getting in her car.

He salutes. "Good morning, Quinn, Grier."

"Good morning, Charles."

I tug open the car door, bend and sit. "Ouch. This seat is hot." I shift so smaller amounts of my thighs touch the leather. "Parked in the driveway last night, did we?" I turn to wave at Charles again.

Grier notices, doesn't put the car in gear, but stops to give me the once over.

I try to be nonchalant. "What? Why are you staring at me?"

"Look at you. It's sweet to see you two together, like kids sharing in the sandbox."

"What are you talking about? I got to bed early after a long soaking bath and slept like a porch dog. Don't give me the third degree." I sit back smugly. Now the warm leather feels comforting.

"*Uh huh*, sure. I'll change the subject to avoid further denials on your part. I like that color on you."

I reach behind to pat the big dog. "Let's do the beach today. I want to walk down to see Eleanor. She rented a furnished condominium across from where she lived."

Grier parks the car with a dozen other cars at the beach circle. We slide our sandals off and toss them back into the car. A landscaping truck and four men are propping another pair of palm trees up with two by four teepees.

"We've come here so much, I forgot how everything used to be, even getting used to seeing the palm trees." I grimace.

"The waves are higher because of the storm." Grier plows her feet into the warm sand. "Feels good. The tide is out. We'll find lots of shells this morning."

The dry sand squeaks against our feet. We power walk along the surf, stopping to pick up shells and trash. Eleanor greets us as she emerges from the waves. She jogs over.

"I must have been a zombie coming from the airport the other day. I apologize for how I acted. Thank you again for the ride." She picks at her hair with her fingers.

"Eleanor, how are you doing?" I ask.

"The insurance company gave me a car since mine was totaled in the blaze. I have several months' rent-free accommodations. I'm feeling much better. Please, come up to the condominium. We'll have ice tea. Besides, I want to show you something."

The remains of Eleanor's home stands against the white dunes. The singed windows on the pale building remind me of eye sockets on a skull. Siding, from the remaining units, twists in melted ribbons.

"It's fortunate my neighbors weren't home this past weekend." Eleanor doesn't glance at her sodden, black furniture or former home.

"Quinn, did you get the copy of our Club information? It would take me quite a while if I had to enter everything by hand again."

I stomp my sandy feet on the boardwalk and follow Eleanor to her new lodgings. "I have a copy of the disk and a bunch of file folders."

"That's a relief."

"There's a copy of the program, too. I don't mind keeping them. You have enough on your mind." My eyes linger on the burned out shell of Eleanor's home.

Begin Again, Quinn

"Come around to the back." She leads us to another set of buildings. "This will do until they rebuild mine. Investigators are still going through the old place." She reaches through the sliding glass door to pick up an object. "I have no idea why anyone would want to burn my home down. It's such an inconvenience. I suppose mischief is mischief. Someone wanted to see a big fire."

She brings a towel wrapped object over to us and sets it on the picnic table. "The fire inspector brought this over last night. I bought it in Sweden a few years ago." She looks at Grier. "Remember? Oh, you didn't go with us. I think it was Kat, Alice and Margaret." She pulls down the towel to reveal a trio of dolphins, riding a wave crest.

"I remember you had this in your dining room hutch," Grier says.

"It's beautiful, isn't it? I was shocked when he handed it to me. It was all sooty. Washing it last night, I felt like a mother giving a bath to her new baby."

"It's beautiful." I reach to stroke the cool smooth glass.

Eleanor heads back to her kitchen once more. She returns wearing a short terrycloth wrap and shower clogs. She carries a tray of tea-filled glasses. She also brings out a bowl of water for Mojo.

"Thank you." I take a sip. "May I?" I pick up the blown glass sculpture with both hands. "I'll never understand how they make these -- it's like ice. Lucky it wasn't broken."

"We watched them make several things and this one caught my eye. I didn't think it would make it home in one piece, but I guess they know how to ship." Eleanor sits with unfocused eyes for a moment.

Grier leans out from the picnic table bench, pulling the dog in to make him sit. He pants and flops down. His wet sandy fur makes a Rohrshack design on the deck. Steam and foam churns on the surface of a tub sitting on a platform.

163

"You have a Jacuzzi here. I bet you'll enjoy it and the outside shower."

"Yes. I enjoy them both. I rinse off the salt in the shower and hop into the warm bubbling water after my swim." She rubs her arms. "These old muscles are beginning to cramp. I may have both a shower and Jacuzzi installed when I rebuild."

Grier says, "Is there anything we can do for you?"

"No, really, thank you. I don't mean to sound rude, but you know by now how I work. I'm fine." She reaches for Grier's hand and mine. She holds them firmly, giving us a comforting tug. "If there's anything else over there, it's beyond rescuing. It's burned, black with soot, or water-soaked. I'm actually looking forward to buying new furniture. I guess every woman wants to throw it all out and start over once." She shrugs, "I wish I could have saved my family pictures." Eleanor faces us from her side of the picnic table and gazes over at the whirlpool. Her mind is beginning to get back to business.

I recognize the stare and tug on Grier. Eleanor isn't used to hugging. When I give her one and pat her back, she stiffens in my embrace.

"I know you have a lot to do today." I console her. "We better start back."

Mojo clumps up and stretches. We step off the porch and walk around the corner of the complex. A bronze Mercedes chugs up, spewing a cloud of black smoke across the parking lot.

"Oh my God," says Grier. "It's Lloyd Batts. Keep your head down."

Like any predator, his head jerks around. I can feel his gaze following us.

"Grier, Grier Dew." His window slides down and he pokes his head out. "I thought I recognized you." He nods over to the ruins. "It's a tragedy, a pure tragedy. It shouldn't have happened. In my insurance business, I see this kind of thing all the time. I bet it was a pot on the stove. Women need to be more careful."

"Excuse me. I don't believe we've met." Lloyd opens the door of his automobile, unfolds his body and extends his right hand. Despite his air-conditioned car, his flushed complexion reveals perspiration sheen. "My name is Lloyd Batts and you are Miss…?" He reaches into his top jacket pocket with his other hand and withdraws a business card.

I ignore the extended hand. "Quinn, Mr. Batts." I turn to pull Grier and Mojo away. "Now you mention it, I may have left something on my stove. Grier, we need to be going. Sorry we can't stay and chat." I hurry off, using my best power walk, elbows and fists flying. "Nice to meet you, Mr. Batts." I give him a hearty wave as we head off.

Out of Batts' sight and earshot, Grier loses control of her giggles. "I can't believe what you did. I've never seen him speechless. Quinn Winslow – one, Lloyd Batts – zero. Wow." She coughs in her laughter. "Lord, but you still surprise me."

"It was awful of me, wasn't it? I could smell his cologne over the burnt rubble and combined with his car's diesel fumes, ugh. Tricia and Alice told me about him. He's a horrible condescending toad!" I brush the sand from my hands with the same ease. "I spared myself the handshake. I could literally smell this one coming."

We return to our shoes, brush our feet off and drive back across the bridge.

Relaxing now, I lean against the car door. "Danny is restless. He's looking at new businesses for the area. He mentioned going down to Myrtle Beach but also Charleston and small towns along the waterway."

"Well, he needs to be looking about, for other things, too, like a girlfriend. He carried the torch for you all these years, maybe he'll find more than a business opportunity while he's gone. Will you miss him?"

"No, I'm glad he finally got the message. I hope he does find something and someone." I shake off that thought. "Here comes Charles to greet us."

Grier steers her Volvo into my driveway and says, "Hello again," to Charles. To me, "See you tomorrow." Grier waves as she backs out.

"I'll call you. I need to go to Raleigh next week." Turning to Charles, "Well," I give him an appreciative eye, "you look all spruced up. New haircut?" I sniff, "I like Old Spice cologne. My father wore it."

"Thank you. I've worn it since I started shaving, as a mere lad." He tries a W. C. Fields impersonation. "I'm off for my annual checkup with Hank Morrison. I have a few errands before I meet him. Need anything?"

I'm on alert. Charles is acting differently. He follows me up to the porch and holds the door while I search for my key.

"*Noooo*, thanks for asking," I look him square in the eyes and he winks. His dark eyes remind me of polished steel. "Why, if I didn't know better, I'd say you were flirting with me. Are you feeling all right?"

"I have never felt better. Is this good flirting? It's been so long, I wasn't sure I was doing it right." He places both hands in his trouser pockets and rocks back on his heels.

"Very nice flirting, Charles." I beam back.

"How about we go out to dinner tonight? I believe the next step is a date. At my age, I can't afford to piddle around. What do you say?" He stands politely holding my door while I ponder.

With the exception of Danny, I haven't been asked out in years. My eyes narrow, "Charles Goodwin. If you think you're going to hoodwink me into believing you want to go out for some chivalrous, save the lady-in-distress reason, you have another think coming." I step into my house.

"I'm shocked," he mocks me. "I want to take you to dinner, Quinn, tonight. I enjoy your company." He runs one hand up and down the door frame while he waits for my answer. "That's a rare statement for me to make to a woman, after all these years of fighting them off. Now, is six o'clock a good time for you? Dress is casual. It won't be fancy, just good food." His years of using an assumptive close in sales gives him the edge.

"Okay, we'll do it. I'm delighted to accept your request." I curtsy. "I accept -- you made a sale. If the food and company are good, how can I refuse?"

Giddy, I peer through the peephole as Charles goes down the steps. Oh, Lord, I have the faith and the hope. I sure hope this isn't charity. My face flushes between my hands. I go into my room to select which clothes I'll wear and then take a shower. I plan to spend the rest of the day on the computer, with a little hair tousling before six.

Charles drives over later. I hurry out my side door into the garage and hit the door opener before he's out of his car. I toss a stack of Eleanor's folders into the car trunk. Everything stowed, purse on my arm, I hit the switch to shut the garage door. Ducking under the closing door, I take his offered hand.

"I'm going to see Eleanor tomorrow morning. I needed to put those folders in my car. I just finished reading it all."

Charles stops. "Is this about your Investment Club investigating? I don't like it, if it is."

"Not to worry, my friend. I'm turning it all over to Sam after I speak to Eleanor." I slide into the seat as he holds the door. "You're such a gentleman, Charles. Thank you. May I ask where we're going?"

"You may. We're going the long way around Beaufort and take the ferry across the Neuse River. There's a family restaurant with excellent shrimp, but you can order

167

anything. You haven't taken the ferry recently, have you?" He smiles when I shake my head.

"I can't tell you how long it's been since I took a ferry."

"Where we're going isn't too far from the landing, Arapahoe."

I sit quietly in the seat, watching the roadside. The Crown Victoria's interior is luxurious compared to my car. I feel enveloped in a gray leather bean bag. We pass through Beaufort and turn onto the narrow country road that stretches through farmlands and eventually over the Core Creek Intracoastal Waterway high-rise bridge.

"Look at all the boats. I had no idea there were this many." I sit up and glance over the bridge to view the waterway below.

"They built this boatyard a while back and each year there are more boats in it," he informs me. "The Coast Guard brings theirs here, so it must be good. Some day I might get a boat. We live on the water, won't have to pay dockage. You think that would be a good idea?"

"I grew up being around boats. You'll enjoy it." My head whips along the fields identifying the soybean and cotton crops. "This area used to be all big farms. Not all of it became housing developments."

We ride in silence a few minutes. "You told me you came from Boston. Why here?" I turn in my seat to focus on his face. He missed one spot shaving. White whiskers make a furry patch by his ear.

"I moved down about twenty years ago. I was stationed at Camp Lejeune when I was in the Marine Corps. I always wanted to come back. When my wife died, I made the move." He taps the electric window button. It opens a bit, allowing the heat and smells of the summer woodlands to filter into the car.

Begin Again, Quinn

Loblolly bays and pines flank the roadside wetlands. The bay's white blossoms glow like Christmas ornaments on the trees.

"You never forget the smells of open country and farmlands." He says. "I often take the ferry over to walk around Oriental. It's a nice village, a bit out of the way. We'll have to visit that another day, when we have more time."

"I know what you mean about the smells of summer. They bring back good memories for me, too. When I was a little girl, my Daddy would pile us into the station wagon on Sunday afternoons. We'd drive all over this county. Sometimes we rode all the way down to Cedar Island. We fed bread to the seagulls.

"For summer vacation, we'd take my father's boat or the ferry over to Ocracoke and camp out. Lord, but they had hungry mosquitoes over there. I suppose all that changed." Lots of childhood memories flood through my mind.

"Well, you don't feed the seagulls on this ferry. It's just a short ride, but the gulls have a reputation for messing up your car or worse you if you stand under them." Charles turns into the road leading to the ferry landing.

While eating, we grow more at ease with one another. We both order shrimp. He gets the fried; I order broiled. He tells me about his childhood, marriage and places where he served in the Marine Corps.

"How'd you get into financial planning?" I ask.

"I had my college degree and after retiring went to one of those job fairs. The company recruited me. I studied and got an advance degree in the business."

"I always thought stocks were risky."

"I educated my clients before I did business with them." He reassures me.

"You gave me a lot of information. The way you explained it was easy to understand."

"Thank you. I became a financial planner at a good time."

He asks me about my life. I tell him about being a daughter, a wife and a divorced young woman working in Raleigh. I share memories about Aunt Grace and my family.

"I appreciate your candor. I want to know more about you, Quinn. You don't have the accent of the locals."

"Funny, after moving back, it doesn't take long to pick it up, especially if I'm around Grier." I refuse the tray of dessert offerings.

The smells of the river, as we ride the ferry back, churn up more feelings. I cling to my past, yet want something new. I can't decide if I want more than friendship with Charles.

As we leave Beaufort behind and drive to the top of the Morehead City high-rise bridge, he slows his car. The full moon is on the horizon over the Sound.

"Oh, it's lovely." My mouth opens in astonishment.

"I thought you'd like it. I checked the paper this morning and noted the full moon. That's another reason I wanted to take you out tonight." He appears very smug.

We don't speak again until Charles parks his car at his home. He walks me back to my house.

"Charles, I've had a lovely evening. Won't you come in for some coffee? I…." Gasping in horror, I peer through the door at my home. "Lord have mercy!"

My furniture is tossed about. Drawers emptied on the floor and closets pulled apart. Staring down the hall, I see broken glass on the floor.

"Come out, Quinn." Charles gently tugs me away. "Someone may still be here. I'll call the police from my house."

Begin Again, Quinn

We quickly walk the distance between houses and within minutes, the police arrive. Two uniformed police officers walk though the house, checking for damage and intruders.

Officer Willis, speaking with a soft local brogue, escorts me into the house. "Would you mind walking through with me? The worst seems to be in the computer room. There are books and pictures thrown around in the back room. The other bedroom was hardly touched."

The young woman senses my apprehension. "Have you lived here long, ma'am?" She talks casually, hoping to draw me out of my shock.

"I was born in the hospital when it was downtown. It's a nursing home now. I grew up here."

The police officer seems young, despite her uniform and gun. The Kevlar vest beneath her shirt gives her a pigeon-chested appearance.

"My mother's silver! It was all stored under the guest bed." The cloth-lined notched drawer of the silver chest gapes at me, like a jack o'lantern. I search around for other missing family treasures but the silverware seems to be the only thing absent.

Charles follows us, shaking his head. "I can't believe the audacity of someone doing this. Was it your ex-husband or do you think this is related to the other attempts on your friends' lives, Quinn?"

"What's that," interrupts Officer Willis. "You think this is related to another incident?"

"Yes, Officer, perhaps you better call Sam Dew. I don't think my former husband would do this."

Charles shakes his head.

"I belong to a group of women who've had a series of bad experiences. One became very ill, one died and another had her home burned down. I believe everything's related." My hand covers my mouth. "Are you familiar with the fire at the beach last weekend? Someone may have burgled Eleanor Aldridge's home before it was set afire. I can't imagine how I would figure in all this. I'm too new to the club.

"I don't think it was Matt." I sink onto my couch and gaze around the Carolina room warily. "I don't keep money in the house." I jump up and find my pickle jar broken on the kitchen floor. I pick up the remaining rim and show it to Charles. "This couldn't have been more than eighty dollars."

The officer makes notes in her notebook.

Grier arrives with Sam. She sits with Charles and me at his house, while police officers search my house. One team looks for an incendiary device, but finds none. When they are through, they let us back inside my home. Grier helps me clean up the mess. Sam and Charles board up the back window. Sam finishes talking with the fingerprint expert.

"They used a sock on the doorknob. Real professional thief," he grins. "If it weren't so close to all the other happenings, I'd think it was a random vandalism and theft." He scratches his head, "We'll check pawn shops and flea malls. This amateur won't remain loose for long."

"Are you sure you don't want to come over to our house tonight?" Grier asks.

I shake my head. "Thanks for offering, but I'm not afraid of sleeping in my own home."

I usher them to the front door. Even though I've replaced many glass windows, I'm relieved when Charles says he'll take care of fixing the window.

It's after midnight. "Do you still want to walk in the morning?" Grier asks.

"I'll want to walk this out of my system. Definitely, let's do it." I rub the back of my neck to relieve the tension.

Once again, in the dark and alone, I walk through every room, checking for locked windows and doors. Exhausted, I slide between the sheets. Would Matt do this?

Begin Again, Quinn

Who else on my list of suspects would break into my home? Why?

Across the garden, the light from Charles' window is reassuring. To my relief, sleep comes quickly.

Karen Dodd

NINETEEN

A bead of sweat forms on my upper lip. The early morning heat causes perspiration to run down my neck and collect on the shirt collar and under my bra. I close my T'ai Chi with the final wave. The past month's events pile up in my mind: remodeling, investment club, Charles, Danny, near death of friends and now the break-in. My mind crashes into a typical roadrunner-coyote pileup. Taking several soothing breaths, I push all thoughts out of my mind and breath in smells of turned earth, roses and a hint of ocean saltiness seasoning the air.

That's when it hits me, like an epiphany, but without angels or bright glaring lights. It's more like melting snow dropping on my head from an overhanging roof.

After all these years, I realize, the only thing worse than marrying my high school boyfriend was keeping my failed marriage alive in my mind. My feelings of guilt and shame fall away like sand pouring out from a sock. Maybe it's the alchemy of a salt breeze mixing with the fragrances of my garden, but "now I know in part, but then I shall know fully…." The Corinthian love verse takes on new meaning. "I did away with childish things." I'm chilled, damp and hot -- all at the same time.

They say a runner's high increases senses. Colors are brighter. Smells and tastes are more distinct. Touch is more sensitive. My epiphany has the same effect. My breakfast bran muffin and coffee taste especially good.

Grier and I walk our short route. After she drops me off, I shower and reheat a cup of coffee in the microwave and finish the crossword puzzle. The phone rings as I'm washing out my cup.

Sam Dew identifies himself. "Quinn, I think we've caught your break-in culprit. I wonder if you can drive down to police headquarters to identify your silverware. She went to two pawn shops this morning. The suspect is a minor and right now she's being held until her grandmother arrives."

I immediately know it's Tomorrow. Somewhat relieved neither Matt nor a "senior citizen killer" is involved; I agree to meet him within the hour. I call Charles and tell him I'm going out, delaying his repair. I also telephone Marguerite Peterson.

"I can't come in today. I'm afraid I have some disturbing news."

She sucks in a breath as I explain about the break-in.

"I suspect they'll be holding Tomorrow. I don't know why she broke into my house or stole from me."

Marguerite says, "That child doesn't have sense enough to avoid the pointy end of a stick."

I hear her digging in her purse for her forbidden pack of cigarettes.

"She's been mostly ignored, hustled around and abused. I'm not letting her sink any further. I'll be downtown when you get there."

I hear the distinctive click of a lighter and her inhaling.

The municipal building is located between the waterfront and the town's main street. In the past twenty years, most businesses have moved out along the highway leading into town or closed, thanks to the super stores. Finding a parking space on the waterfront, I walk back and greet Marguerite as she pulls her car into a handicapped space at the front door.

"It didn't take you long to get here." She hooks a handicapped tag onto her mirror and helps an elderly woman out of the car. "This is Macie Campbell, Tomorrow's grandmother."

I shake her cold hand, noting the fire in her eyes.

"I'm taking a switch to that girl. It's her Mama's wildness. I tried to beat it out of her but she's a stubborn little thing. Miss Quinn, I'm sorry for what she did."

Before I can respond, Sam opens the front door and invites us inside the building. "She admits to taking the silver and some change, but says the door was open when she got there." He raises his eyebrows.

After introducing both women to Sam, I glance up to see an officer leading Tomorrow.

"I didn't break into your house!" Her short pink skirt barely covers her thighs. The shirred midriff blouse accents her small breasts. Her eyes smolder with the same fire I noted in her grandmother's. She hops around her guard, arms flying and shaking her frizzy mane.

"The door was already open, I say. Somebody else busted the window and tore up your house. Glass all over the place. See. I cut myself when I went in." She pulls a dirty foot out of her shoe. Blood tracks down her ankle and a dry smear dirties the heel. "You the one caused me this trouble." She points a thin finger at me. "It's always you!"

The grandmother slaps her face. "You hush. Don't say no more, you hear?"

Tomorrow slits her eyes, presses her lips together and glares.

Mrs. Campbell turns from Sam to Marguerite. "What we have to do now?"

Sam divides the party, sending Marguerite, Mrs. Campbell and Tomorrow down the hall with the officer. He leads me into another room.

"Sorry. I've called Social Services and the Child Advocates. She admits to robbing you. I need you to...."

"Sam, I don't want to press charges." I'm gritting my teeth. "She's had a terrible life. Is there a way we can get her away from here? Maybe, place her in a home. I don't want her to go to prison because she took my mother's silver. Are there other options?"

"She won't go to prison."

I identify my pillowcase and the silverware. He makes a note to return the evidence.

"Do you have time for me to ask a couple of questions before I leave?" I ask.

He sits on the corner of his desk and folds his hands together. "What now?"

"Humor me for a minute. Do police departments keep up with accidental deaths?" I formed my list of questions on the drive down. "I'll take short answers and don't stop me from hypothesizing."

"No, our county doesn't. I don't know of anyone else who does."

"Do you call in a medical examiner for accidental deaths? Are there autopsies?"

"Our medical examiner is not used for accidental deaths. If the investigating officers or coroner feels it warrants additional evaluation, yes, we do more. Quinn, what are you talking about?"

I interrupt him. "Would you know if there are any ongoing investigations by the insurance commissioner down here?"

He sighs, "We aren't usually called in unless foul play is suspected and no, I know of none." He's tiring of my questions. "Quinn, I need to know."

I grab my purse and stand up. "Don't know anything yet. Thank you. I'll continue to mull all this over and if I come up with anything, I'll call you. Give my love to Grier. I guess I'll see her tomorrow morning."

"Don't run off. There are forms to sign."

Within the hour, I'm outside breathing in the smells of fried seafood from nearby restaurants and marsh along the waterfront. The morning's events weigh on my mind.

Stressful events, at one time, drove me to the Dairy Queen or a bakery. Instead, I walk the four blocks to Bridges Book. Browsing books will take my mind off the present. The fresh flowers, smell of new books and a mug of good coffee will calm me. Danny is behind the computer screen in the workroom.

"I'm glad you're here," I say. "I'm having a disconcerting day. Your store makes me feel good. Mind if I browse while I drink up your coffee?"

"Delighted you came into my humble shop, Madame. Allow me to make you a fresh pot of coffee. One moment, I shall conjure my favorite blend, if you will."

I need to hear kind, light hearted words. Danny mixes Dickens with Shakespeare and throws in a bit of Emeril. I put my bag on a nearby stool as he closes down his web search. He swings around and hops off his perch.

"I'll brew you up a mild Samoan blend. Let me know if I can do anything to make you feel more welcome." He's being absurd and ridiculous, but I like it. He pours beans from a bag, grinds and scoops them into the filter. The aroma and watching him, settles my nerves. I enjoy him fussing over me.

"Don't let me keep you from your work. I'm sure you have more to do than stand here and talk." I chuckle at his antics.

"Nope, my job is to keep the customer happy. I'm at your service." He folds his arms across his flowered shirt.

With sandaled feet, his relaxed Jimmy Buffet look makes me smile. I can't resist his charm. While sitting in the cluster of chairs, I dump everything going on, including my stack of clipped obituaries and the story of Tomorrow. He listens while I sink back into the cushioned chair, prop up my feet and enjoy his attention.

"And this neighbor of yours, Charles. I bet there is more than neighborliness developing." He gently probes.

"I don't know and I can't explain anymore but it feels right. Can you understand?"

"I'm afraid I do. I'm getting second place once more." He shrugs remembering my attraction for Matthew. "We're still good friends, though?"

"Of course."

"Then I'll have to settle for that, unless you change your mind."

With Charles, I'm still cautious about what I share, but with Danny my problems melt with each tick of the clock. When another customer comes in, Danny jumps up. I refill my coffee and flip through a stack of books on the table.

Nancy walks through the store, rearranging a teapot and pulling brown leaves from the potted plants. She smiles in my direction without really seeing me. The evening stream of customers drifting in from nearby restaurants prompts me to give my thanks, find my purse and leave. I didn't realize I had been there all afternoon. I buy a couple of books before leaving.

TWENTY

The Monday following my break-in dawns sunny with a brisk wind. The morning temperature is already over seventy degrees when Grier honks her horn. I walk out onto my porch, greet Charles who's working in his garden and join Grier.

"Let's hope this good weather lasts a while, although I enjoy hot steamy August thunderstorms when they come." I sink into the familiar leather seat, taking deep breaths, shoving the previous week's conflict and resolutions out of my mind. "I've almost got my glass bowl filled with shells. Can we do the beach again this morning?"

"Sure, Mojo tends to be more settled after our beach walks. The water and sand give him a better workout."

Grier rattles on in a friendly way. I think she's trying to avoid any topic leading to the break-in, attempted murder or Matt.

"Let's go down to Ft. Macon today. It shouldn't be as crowded as the main beach. I'll give you my spiel about the fort. I use it when I volunteer as a docent. You've never seen me in my Civil War costume. Remind me to show it to you."

She leans back on her headrest, "Ft. Macon was built in the early 1800's. Hidden in the natural foliage of the island forest, it was surveyed by Robert E. Lee, an Army Engineer in the 1840's and later used by the Confederate forces to defend the Beaufort Inlet during the Civil War." She pauses.

"Don't stop. I'm enjoying this. Continue."

"Today the fort's been restored and is one of the most visited state parks in the nation. Anglers, picnickers and walkers prefer its seclusion." She breaks her heavily accented Southern delivery. "Remember the old concrete bunkers they used in World War II? The dunes have changed, but they're still there."

Begin Again, Quinn

I close my eyes listening to her voice. It helps me to relax during her erratic driving. When the car slows, I open my eyes. The Atlantic Ocean peeks between two sand dunes on the winding beach road. Grier takes the last curve like a bobsledder and brakes entering the visitors' parking area.

"We can walk down to the breakwater and go west along the shore," she suggests. "See? They've done a lot with the old fort since we were girls."

"The welcome center and Coast Guard station are a lot bigger than I remember." I stand on the sandy walkway leading down to the beach. The wind whips my blouse and pants. A violent surf crashes onto the rocky breakwater. The fine mist sprays us as we climb down the timbered steps.

We pick our way to the shoreline through the dunes. After walking for fifteen minutes to a deserted area, Grier loosens Mojo from his leash. He takes off to chase birds scurrying among the waves.

"Oh, he loves this. My only regret is the mess he makes in the car. When we get home, I'll hose him down and let him dry in the sun on the back porch."

With the sun and wind on our backs, we follow the excited dog. The shelling is better in this area. As I find new and better shells, I rinse them off in the surf and drop them into my mesh bag. We updated our uniform for shelling since the first walk with the plastic grocery bags. Our pockets hold tissue and lip gloss. We made net bags for shell and trash collection. The booming waves mesmerize us until Mojo's loud barking attracts our attention.

"What's Mojo barking at?" Grier shields her eyes.

In the distance, the surf has thrown up large pieces of driftwood. The dog runs back and forth, barking at something. Seaweed and foam lap at the ocean's rejects. We quicken our pace to investigate. He gallops between the tidal pool and us. As we approach, we discover a body.

"Oh, my God, someone's drowned in this surf. Why would anyone dare to swim here alone?" Grier holds her dog while I look closer.

I feel like I've had the air knocked out of me. "It's Eleanor." Holding both knees with my hands, I bend over until the nausea passes. "She's dead," I whisper.

"The current must have towed her down the beach." Greir crouches beside me. "If you stay here, I'll go back and get help. Do you mind? My cell phone's in the car. Hold Mojo."

I sit on the damp sand holding the leash, now clipped firmly to the dog's collar. He circles and sinks down, putting his head close to my feet. I dig my toes into the sand trying to warm them. Mojo rests his head on top of them, sharing his body heat. I start to shiver, more from shock than the brisk wind.

Grier turns and jogs straight up through the dunes. The soft sand slows her steps. I watch every foot fall, afraid to glance at our dead friend. When she reaches the top, Grier climbs over the rail fence along the beach road. A car slows to her wave and she climbs in.

###

By noon, we're back at my home. Mojo rests on my porch with a bowl of water as we sit in the kitchen.

"This is a nightmare and I can't wake up." I feel churned like the ocean we left. While I sit at my breakfast bar, Grier fills the teapot with fresh water and turns on the range.

Before the water can boil, Charles taps on the door. He's brought a new piece of glass and a parcel of tools and supplies. I invite him in, offer him tea and tell him about our morning. He listens, sitting erect. All his soldier awareness returns. I see him visually check out our surroundings, as if an enemy might infiltrate my kitchen.

Ending my description of the morning, I say, "She knew the surf. Remember, she even joked about it the first day we met. Sam said they'd have to wait on the medical examiner's report. What's to tell? The surf swallowed her up this morning and she drowned." I sip at my tea. "That dear woman is dead. I wanted to see her today. I had a question to ask about one of her folders. You remember, Charles, I put them in the car the other night. I forgot about them until this morning."

Charles says, "Quinn, you can't do anymore. When you finish your tea, I need your help replacing the window glass. I took the liberty of getting you dead bolts for all your doors. Do you feel up to a bit of maintenance work?"

I know he's trying to take my mind off things. Grier begs off and leads her dog to her car. I pick up the bowl of water from the front porch, rinse it and place it in my dishwasher. Charles waits patiently for me to follow him down the hall.

He lays his tools and glass on a drop cloth. The window molding on the door separates easily. Working, I feel the muscles relax in my neck and shoulders.

"This kind of work comforts me." I sit back leaning against the wall to tug at the glass caulking. "I think I should have been a boy."

"I'm glad you're not," Charles says.

"But I was always helping Daddy when I should have been inside helping Mama. I liked watching him in his workshop."

By late afternoon, I finish sweeping up all the wood shavings. "There, it looks good, Charles, thanks. If you don't mind, I think I'll go lie down. I don't feel like eating or I'd offer to fix us something."

"No problem. I think you'll feel better if you take a nap. With the break-in, the problem with your former husband and this death today, your system's overloaded. Let me fix us something later. Come over when you get up. I'll cook." Charles gathers his tools and leaves.

Karen Dodd

That evening he grills cheese sandwiches and stirs up a creamy tomato-vegetable soup. "Comfort food is what you need. I grew the squash, beans and corn. He blends the tomatoes into a puree and adds them to the pot as he stirs. "Now sit and relax. I hope you like jazz, that's all I have."

His brown leather couch holds me like a coddled egg. I close my eyes listening to the music.

###

The winds picked up as Eleanor climbed through the dunes after her late night swim. Her damp body cooled in the night air. She hurried along the boardwalk to the back of her rental unit. Cold water blasted out of the shower head. Stepping back to avoid the initial spray, she held out a testing hand. When it warmed, she leaned in with closed eyes. Eleanor rinsed the sand from her hair, letting the water wash over her body.

She pulled the cover from the Jacuzzi and climbed in. Her body eased beneath the hot, swirling water until only her face floated above the surface. The day's mental exercise with insurance people and replacing lost items exhausted both her mind and body. She called the children earlier in the evening and talked for an hour.

His strong hands reached out to her shoulders. She grabbed his wrists. Her mouth filled with water as he pushed her head down. Her arms reached up, but within minutes, they fall beneath the surface.

No one saw him drop her body into the surf. The ocean remembered her many years of swimming as the waves cradled her body into the outgoing tide.

TWENTY-ONE

I drive the following day. Sam's still at home when I arrive. He invites me inside. He pulls a chair from their breakfast nook. "I wanted you to go over a few things with me, if you don't mind? This isn't going to be easy." He waits until I sit down. "Eleanor was murdered. Her lungs contained chlorinated water."

"No, how horrible!" I picture Eleanor at her breakfast table looking out at the ocean and smiling at me. This news amplifies my loss. "How can I help you?" I look at Grier. "I know it's all related somehow."

"What do you suspect?" Sam nudges me for my thoughts.

"The survival clause in the Golden Girls' Club is a strong motive. Have you checked out all the members of the club or that nephew of Katherine's?"

"I'm looking at alibis. As for the nephew, he seems to have big financial problems. We pulled an Equifax report on him. He admits being at the country club the day Kat took ill. The night of the fire, he has no alibi."

"I've been keeping a collection of all the accidental deaths of people who died in the past few months, Sam."

"This was no accident, so that blows your theory on accidental deaths. There are bruises on Eleanor's neck and shoulders. Someone held her down until she drowned." Sam sits back on the bench seat and watches my reaction.

"*Ooooh*, Sam. It might have something to do with a company both Kat and Eleanor investigated." I push my chair back. "I'm driving to Raleigh tomorrow morning for a training meeting. Help & Hands appointed me to the Board of Directors. After the meeting, I intend to research companies popping up with some of my accidental death victims."

I explain about the KBM Company which bought Katherine's life insurance policies with accidental death riders, as well as, the reverse mortgage companies who own properties that Tricia grudgingly researched for me. "Eleanor was interested in KBM." I mention the conversation during the church covered dish dinner. I remind Grier of what Tricia told us about Margaret Byrd's home. "Again it could be a coincidence, but they seem related to me."

"A basket of obituaries and a death discussed at a church covered dish supper aren't murders. This is a completely different situation. Can't you understand?" Sam, obviously perplexed by the case and concerned about us, says, "And besides, no one would have the audacity to kill so many people. There would be a money trail as wide as Interstate 40. You're stretching your imagination to connect the dots, don't you think? I believe it's someone in your club or the nephew. Matt cleared out of town, by the way. I checked him out first thing."

I remind him of the recently convicted nurse in a small Oregon town, who killed so many of his patients.

He presses, "This is Carteret County, remember. We have minor crime and a bit of drug trafficking. No serial killers." Sam hesitates, but then asks, "Do you still have the information Kat gave you?"

"Yes. You want to see it?"

He stands up, clipping his cell phone on his belt, grabs his jacket and prepares to leave. "There's no hurry in getting it to me. I have a two-day meeting in Jacksonville and won't get back until late tomorrow."

"It's on my nightstand at home. I took it out of the car to read again. It'll probably put me to sleep tonight. I found Eleanor's folder on KBM and I'm trying to decipher her notes. I'll drop it by your office, Sam. Is late tomorrow afternoon okay? I should be there by four."

"You do that, but nothing else, you hear? I don't want either of you to do anything else." He waggles his index finger. "Keep your doors locked and be aware of what's going on around you." He kisses Grier and leaves.

Grier stands and jangles the leash. "Time's a wasting. There's nothing we can do, Quinn. Let's get on with our walk. I have a dog needing a bath." With the mention of 'bath', Mojo dodges out of Grier's reach. She corners him between her legs and snaps on the lead.

"There you go, big guy. Want to go for a walk?" She explains, "He'll forget I mentioned it while we walk, but I don't advise you to hang around afterwards. He can get real nasty when I start with you-know-what."

We silently walk the lanes around the golf course noting the summer flowers in yards and how the neighborhood changed since our high school days. Later, I drive to the Help & Hands Center and work off my frustrations, sanding down a chest of drawers.

"Someone sure stirred up your energy today," Marguerite says, nodding at all the dust and the sanded drawers.

"Have you heard from Tomorrow?" I wipe dust from my nose.

The teenager's absence makes the work easier for the rest of the women in my class, but her slouched ghost remains in the corner.

"I called her home and got no answer," Marguerite comments. "Macie tells me the girl ran away. Said she was going to Atlanta. Who does she know there?"

I shake my head as she walks away. Hours later, I decide to go home and clean up. By the time I shower, all I want is a large cup of soothing tea, a place to prop up my feet and a clear view of the water.

I get up earlier the next morning. After T'ai chi, I shower, dress and collect my papers for the Raleigh trip. The familiar three-hour drive allows me to reexamine the sequence of events, the deaths and all the people involved. Jessica Fletcher would be proud of me.

Tricia knows real estate value and is successful. Is she too successful? What about her partner, Grady? I don't like Daphne. If she steals, can she kill? Kat's nephew seems like a frustrated young man. Maybe he's trying to cover his tracks in his land development. Certain real estate corporations keep appearing on transfer of ownerships. I need to know the principals of the real estate and insurance corporations.

Attending the domestic abuse meeting, I can't keep my mind on the discussions. Faces of Kat, Eleanor and Tomorrow float by as I scribble lists in the margin of the meeting agenda. Afterwards, I drive downtown and find a

parking space near the Secretary of State building. It's
located across from the old Capitol. The old building had been
a former Department of Revenue Office. Marble walls and
steep steps take me to a uniformed guard's station.

"Could you tell me where I'd go to look up a
company incorporated in North Carolina?"

The imposing uniformed man asks me for a picture
ID and tells me to sign-in. He indicates the woman behind a
bank-like railing.

After waiting in line, I explain my quest. "I want to
know how to find the owners or directors of a corporation in
North Carolina."

I feel I'm asking too much of the busy woman, but am
delighted when she returns my smile. She motions me to
another portion of the teller section.

"If you can wait a minute while I finish with these
gentlemen and check in the mail, I'll have time to help you."

The attractive woman's nametag reads Lisa
Singleton. She helps a couple complete a form. She redirects a
pile of mail with another courier. "Now, what is the name of
the company?"

"It's KBM Incorporated. Here's a list of companies. I
want to know who is involved."

She reads over the list and keys between two
computer screens.

"I don't really know what I'm looking for until I see
it. I drove here from Morehead City. It may be a wild goose
chase."

Several sheets slide out of a nearby printer.

"There seem to be several companies involved. You
read this while I pull up the next few listings." Her slender
dark fingers dance over the keyboard. "What a jungle this one
is. You'd think they were trying to hide something."

Begin Again, Quinn

The woman knows her business. She continues to type. Finally, several dozen printouts pile into the printer bin.

I glance over the sheets. Listed on each corporate page are the company name, address, principals involved and nature of business. As the woman hands me more reports I link names to partnerships and more corporations, sifting out the results.

"Miss Singleton, you've been very helpful. How much do I owe you?" I reach for my purse.

"Nothing, this is a free service. Did you find what you needed?" She glances over to the counter where several people are waiting. "Next time you need information, you can look all this up on the internet. Go to our website and you won't have to drive to Raleigh."

"I learn something new every day. Oh, yes, yes, I did find out what I wanted to know. Thank you so much." During the three-hour drive back to Morehead City, I fail in my quest for both a clean bathroom and a working roadside telephone. I make up my mind to get a cell phone. My intention is to drive straight to Sam's office, but home is on the way.

The garage door rises when I tap the visor-mounted opener. Entering through the kitchen door, I hurry up the hall for a much needed visit to the bathroom. After washing my hands, I turn to find an uninvited guest.

"Good evening, Miss Quinn. You've been a busy woman. Thanks for leaving the garage door open." Lloyd Batts points his cell phone at me as I back into the Carolina room. "*Uh-uh*, now you don't want to do anything foolish." He lifts the folders on KBM and the printouts from Raleigh.

"Look what I found. I looked for these the other night. You hid them too well." He holds his cell phone up. "See this. It's not what you think. It's a stun gun, readily available to Internet shoppers for personal defense. Now, Tricia tried to run off. Will you behave or am I going to have to demonstrate my toy?"

I back up against the wall. "What's Tricia got to do with this?"

"She's a busybody, like your friend, Eleanor and you. You wouldn't let it go. Please turn around, so I can tape your hands." His cell phone taps between my shoulder blades as I wait for the jolt. He picks a roll of duct tape off my kitchen counter. After he wraps my wrists, he pushes me down the hall, though the kitchen door and shoves me into the back seat of my own car. His aftershave reeks. Now, I recall the sweet smell from Eleanor's home.

"Lloyd, I figured out your scam and others are right behind me." I try to sound brave.

Anger turns his facer redder than its normal glow. "Do you think I'm stupid?" His eyes slit and his chin juts out. "Take this." He points the stun gun in my direction.

I try to dodge. The jolt stops the scream in my throat. My body burns with sensations blasting at every nerve ending.

He taunts me. "Keep your remarks to yourself or I may trigger it again." Lloyd shifts the front seat back, scrunching me tighter in my narrow space. He carefully reverses my car out of the garage. "Want to know how this all started?"

He smugly explains. "You see, I'm really a clever fellow. It all started back when I had a partner.

"Good old Ken McNeill." He brags, looking in the rear view mirror to make sure I'm listening.

My ears hear his cruel story while my body jerks to the tune of his stun gun. "Selling personal property and life insurance policies isn't very exciting. Now the reverse mortgages and buying back life insurance policies is a gambler's game. We both enjoyed a gamble. Sure, we sold for real companies, but I set up our own and did the same thing. Setting up dummy corporations is easy. Unless someone has an inquisitive mind," he sends a cold gaze back at me, "there *is* no way to trace us.

Begin Again, Quinn

"Ken was happy. At first, he had no idea what was going on." He bangs the driving wheel with his palm. "Some of our special clients had homes to trade for lifetime income and others didn't even know what the "ADD Rider" meant on their insurance policy. When they died, we had their homes to sell, debt free. For those old codgers who wanted cash for old life insurance policies, well, accidental death pays us more."

I gurgle a low growl, but he can't hear over his boasting.

"Heck, old people die. The medical examiner and Insurance Commissioner's office have enough on their hands. They'd never put it all together, not with all the corporations we use."

"How could you?" My woozy lips form the words. Some feeling returns to my jaw and shoulder.

"Money, my dear. Talk about making a killing in the market! I sold enough of the real policies so no one would be suspicious. I'm very selective. We never sold the 'special policies' to anyone young. *Caveat emptor*. This latest one, Katherine Knowles, had too many friends interested in what she was doing. You and Eleanor and Tricia Lewis, what is it with you girls?"

"We're friends, good friends."

"Too good for your own good." He laughs. He continues his gruesome tale. "Did you know I'm building a new high-rise on the beach? It takes money, a lot of money. I'm a very rich man, thanks to this business, killer profits." His hee-haws ring in my ears.

I shake my head as a cruel laugh chills me to the bone.

"Yeah, special clients meet their Maker sooner." He licks his lips and smiles back at me. "There's so many ways to kill an old person. Can you imagine? After I found this stun gun on the internet, things got easier. It leaves no mark!" He drops the stun gun on the seat beside him.

"Ken exploded the day he came across my special client notebook. Ah, generous Ken left me all that money. I bet he forgot about our buy-sell agreements when he headed his car into the ditch. On the other hand, maybe he didn't do it on purpose. Maybe it was an *accident*." He wipes his face with a handkerchief he pulls from his rear pocket.

I twist my neck to see where he's driving. The small back seat is uncomfortable, especially having my hands taped behind my back. With no feeling in my legs, they're hard to move. A thousand pins prick my soles when I press down trying to turn around.

We cross the bridge to Atlantic Beach and turn toward the western end of the island. His boasting finally ends.

"You're a monster." When I verbalize my thoughts, he zaps me a second time. I feel the surge hit my neck and shoulder. My face goes numb. Fortunately, I can't feel the total force, because the first blast hasn't worn off. My head falls against the window, as my jaw drops open. After thirty minutes, he turns into a steep driveway lined with live oaks and cedars. Opening the door, he pulls me out.

Lloyd steers me around the house, across a patio and pool area and down a long dock. I stumble trying to keep up. He shoves open a door to a boathouse built over the water. While he tapes my ankles together, I discover another form across the room.

"You ladies don't go anywhere. I seem to have acquired several vehicles I need to get rid of" he lowers his voice Terminator-style, "but I'll be back. I'm thinking a late evening boat ride, eh?" He brays again, jostling me over to the side as he pulls the door shut.

"Quinn?" Tricia hoarsely calls across the room. "How bad are you?"

As my eyes focus, I see our bindings are identical.

Begin Again, Quinn

"I've been here all afternoon calling for help. Voice is gone," she whispers. "Quinn, can you move?"

The sun-warmed building pops with the heat. Water splashes below and seagulls screech overhead. A fishy odor penetrates the boathouse.

I roll over. "*Ohhh*, how did you end up here? Where are we?" Pain surrounds my whole body. As I turn to scrunch up into sitting position, I hit my head on a shelf. "*Ouch*. How did Lloyd connect you to this?"

Tricia rouses herself into sitting position. "I called him, remember? I didn't know it was him. You asked me to find out who was selling all those homes. I found a number in the courthouse."

"I don't know which is worse, the initial hit from his stunner or the coming out of it." I struggle to shake off the burning in my shoulders and legs. "Are you still hurting? Tell me how you got here while I sizzle through the pain."

"Earlier this afternoon after I left my office for an appointment, I got a cancellation. Then my beeper says I have a meeting at this house for a listing.

"Here I was thinking my green silk pantsuit was going to make a good impression, checking my makeup and rehearsing my presentation. I didn't think anything was wrong until I didn't get an answer at the front door." She props herself against some boat cushions. "I heard his voice. My warning bells went off." She swallows. "I let out a yell but there was no one to hear. He taped me up and pulled me out here. Guess he thought with the screaming gulls on this lonely stretch, no one would notice." She winds her head slowly around. "Cy Karchetti owns this house. Having all afternoon to think about it, I remember he was in something with both Ken McNeill and Lloyd back when I was first getting into real estate."

I say, "Karchetti is the "K" in KBM. I looked up a bunch of corporations. Lloyd sells reverse mortgage policies and then he kills the policy owners with help from his stun gun. He arranged Margaret Byrd's death to look like an

193

accident. He's been getting away with murder since before Alice's husband died.

"No!" She exclaims. "Is that what this is all about?"

"Gullible people sign over their homes for a life-time income. He had a gold mine as long as they all died within the first years of the policy.

"Margaret must have bought one of those reverse mortgages and Katherine sold her life insurance policy to one of his bogus companies. Dave Paterson's brother swapped his house for a lifetime-income." I continue relaying what I know. "Eleanor was investigating it all. He killed her."

"How did you put this all together?" Tricia elbows herself in my direction.

"I found the link while looking at some of Eleanor's folders. I picked them up by mistake the night I went over. She made notes in the margin about the KBM initials but I couldn't figure them out until today."

"I always knew Batts was a sleaze, but never thought he was a murderer!"

"Eleanor's folder is probably what Lloyd was looking for when he broke into my house. He was in Eleanor's house the night of the fire." I take a deep breath. My T'ai Chi breathing helps me to focus.

Tricia points with her chin to the wall. Our pocketbooks hang on a nail beside the door. "My purse is up there with a cell phone. I've tried standing up but I can't get my balance with my hands behind me." Tricia grimaces, "My guess is we're leaving by the boat tied to this dock. From the looks of things, he doesn't intend on anyone finding our bodies." Tricia kicks a pair of cement blocks tied with a jumble of rope. "He'll take us out and dump us. I scoured this place for a sharp nail or something to tear at the tape. Do you think if we turned you could reach my wrists?"

Begin Again, Quinn

As the burning sensation wanes, I gain control over my arms and legs. "The Lord helps those who help themselves." I scoot toward her.

We wiggle on the floor straining to get our hands together. Our struggling only makes the tape tighter. "Wait, I think one of my rings is catching something. Can you feel it?"

I bite my lip, while sawing against her jewelry. Eventually the duct tape begins to pull apart. I pull one hand free and turn to work on Tricia's hands.

"Don't do me yet. Grab my purse, the cell phone."

I hop over to the wall and find her phone. After I call 911, I turn back to my friend and loosen her hands. In the darkness, we work to pull the sticky bindings from our feet.

We hear a cough and steps vibrate the dock. Each approaching step brings disaster to our short freedom. My heart feels squeezed up into my ears.

From the window, we see him lugging a large suitcase and a shoulder bag. The full moon casts an eerie light around the dock.

"*Shhh*, see he has a gun. Lie back down." I drop to the floor in darkness. "Pretend we're still tied up."

The boat's engine starts. Exhaust fumes invade the small building, burning my eyes and nose. Lloyd revs the big motor and then returns it to idle.

Cautiously, he enters swinging his gun from side to side. "Ah, still here I see. I thought you might plan some little trick." He sneers, "Did you miss me?"

Lloyd sticks the gun into his waistband, lifts our purses down from the nail and throws them into the waiting boat. "After I dump you, I'm taking a ride down to Wrightsville Beach. It's a beautiful night for a boat ride. Well, Miss Quinn and Tricia, we need to be going. I have a plane to catch."

Tricia eyes me, waiting for a signal. Lloyd picks up one concrete block and places it in the stern of the boat. He turns to lift the other. At my nod, we both jump, pushing him towards the boat. He steps back, dropping the cement block as his hands fly out for balance. I hear a crack and a splash as his body bangs against the stern of the boat.

Keeping my balance, I spin, pushing Tricia back toward the building. I almost follow Lloyd. My one leg is flung over the water but I shift my weight back on the other foot. T'ai Chi weight shift and balance keep me upright. Sirens in the distance wail their approach. We lean against the boat house, waiting while our breathing and heart rates to return to normal.

###

He falls near the stern of the boat, arms churning the water. Lloyd sinks below the surface. His hands reach to loosen the weighted nylon line tightening around his ankles. Dredged to a depth of fifteen feet, the slip beside the dock on high tide now gulps twenty feet of water above the mud-sucking bottom. He lunges, trying to pull himself up. Blood pours from cuts on his fingers as he clutches at the barnacle-covered pilings. As Lloyd's lungs fill with water, some trick of his mind flashes faces, like a photo album of his special clients. The water stills.

###

I climb aboard the big boat, turn off the engine and gather up our purses. Unprompted, another Bible verse floats off my lips, "In the net which they hid, their own feet have been caught."

"What did you say?" Tricia slides down the side of the building to sit on the dock.

"It's a verse from Psalms. Something I memorized years ago."

The dock bounces with running feet. Shouts echo across the water.

"Quinn, are you all right?" Charles reaches out. "When I heard you were missing, I joined the search."

Begin Again, Quinn

An officer helps Trish stand and walk toward shore. Several people in uniforms pass us on their way out to the boathouse.

Sitting on the backyard patio, I see them dip a boat hook into the water. The images form a surreal impression. Shadows move against the dock-house. A marsh hen screams into the night. Clouds glide across the moon.

They grapple Lloyd and haul up his body. A wet line falls back into the water, along with a shoe. The beam of artificial light shines on his pale foot. A gruesome reminder -- it could have been us.

The phone rings. For a brief moment, I forget the previous night. The doctor at the hospital gave me a sleeping pill. Glancing at my clock, I note the time.

"Hello. Grier? Yes, I want to walk." I roll over to sit up. "*Oooh*, I ache from muscles I never knew I had."

Grier's excited drawl revives me, "Sam didn't get home until a couple of hours ago. They found a notebook of all of Lloyd's victims. You won't believe what he did."

"I don't want to hear about it. It's over. Give me another hour so I can get up and eat. I'll drive and no, I don't want to walk on the beach!"

"It's a date. See you then, Honey." She hangs up.

I gaze out the window watching Charles bend in his garden, weeding between his squash and cucumbers. Sliding the window open wider, I lean against the frame. "Good morning, Charles. Have you had breakfast?"

He straightens. "No, I was waiting on you. I have some strawberries. Do you still have some of that good bread?"

"It'll be toasted by the time you clean up." I head for the bathroom.

Searching the closet, I pull out a purple shirt and shorts. My hair only needs a finger run-through, a tousle.

The coffee drips into the carafe. Pulling a loaf of Mrs. Doerr's sweet, yeasty bread from its wrappings, I slice two large hunks and slather them with whipped butter before sliding them into the toaster oven.

I hum, stacking blackberry preserves, plates and mugs on a tray. After I pour two glasses of orange juice, I fold cloth napkins and place a knife and spoon on top.

"Ms. Winslow, are you decent?" Charles taps at my front door.

Walking around the kitchen island, I greet him, "Now Charles, I told you to call me Quinn. We're neighbors now and it's okay to use first names."

He laughs a deep, wonderful laugh and draws me into his arms.

———————

Begin Again, Quinn

Acknowledgements

A big thank you to my cousin Bill Ramseur, MD, my brother-in-law, Steve Langham for arson information, daughter, Christine Grotheer for her editing pickiness and my husband, Denton Dodd for his support. A family willing to tolerate my moodiness, questions and schedules is one of my greatest blessings.

Other people include Secretary of State employee, Linda Singleton. She had the patience to help me delve into corporate identities. The NC Coalition Against Domestic Violence explained NC domestic abuse laws. A docent volunteer, reached through the website, answered my Ft. Macon questions. David Billingsley, Billingsley Security explained tasers and stun guns. Dear friends, Rosie Wood gave me suggestions and Joan Smith, became a role model for my active "mature" ladies. She's 92 and I can't keep up with her.

My critique groups members read and helped juggle words of this story: Eileen Cella, Eileen Myers, Kay Parker, Ruth Russell, Gloria Russakov, Qaey Williams and Katherine Wolfe. My writing coaches, Maxine Harker and Richard Krawiec helped with portions of this book. Thank you and thank you.

I used some real names of people and businesses - with their permission. If someone else finds his or her name here, it's purely coincidence. Any error in information is entirely my own. Bits and pieces of my former financial planning clients seeped into my scenes, especially my PKS ladies. They shared their friendship, golf games and bridge playing-during-hurricane stories with me.

Coastal North Carolina is close to my heart. I've lived here most of my life.

Karen Dodd

All books are available from the publisher. If you would like a book, copy this page and mail to:

KE Dodd

6304 Albatross Dr.

New Bern, NC 28560

		Quantity	Total
Carolina Comfort	$12.95	_____	_____
Carolina Comfort II	12.95	_____	_____
Down East	12.95	_____	_____
Begin Again, Quinn	12.95	_____	_____
SUBTOTAL COST			_____
Repeat Buyers 15% discount	--		_____
Total Cost of books			_____
Shipping and Handling $2/book			-----------------
Make check out for Total			===========

THANK YOU!

CPSIA information can be obtained at www.ICGtesting.com
Printed in the USA
BVOW030256160212

282987BV00001B/5/A